ricochet

ALSO BY JULIE GONZALEZ

Wings

ricochet

JULIE GONZALEZ

DELACORTE PRESS

Published by Delacorte Press
an imprint of Random House Children's Books
a division of Random House, Inc.
New York

www.randomhouse.com/teens

Educators and librarians, for a variety of teaching tools, visit us at
www.randomhouse.com/teachers

Library of Congress Cataloging-in-Publication Data

Gonzalez, Julie.
Ricochet / Julie Gonzalez. —1st ed.
    p. cm.
    Summary: When his best friend is killed in a game with a loaded gun, fifteen-year-old
Conner finds his perceptions of himself and his relationships with his family, friends,
and the other people in his life changed in more profound ways than he could have
imagined.
    ISBN 978-0-385-73228-4 (trade) — ISBN 978-0-385-90254-0 (Gibraltar lib. bdg.)
    [1. Firearms—Fiction. 2. Best friends—Fiction. 3. Friendship—Fiction.
4. Brothers—Fiction. 5. Guilt—Fiction. 6. Conduct of life—Fiction.] I. Title.
PZ7.G593Ric 2007
[Fic]—dc22
2006024348

The text of this book is set in 12-point Goudy.
Book design by Kenny Holcomb

Printed in the United States of America

10 9 8 7 6 5 4 3 2 1

First Edition

To Carl, my youngest child,
and Anna Tringas,
his violin instructor

This story was born at the foot of
Mrs. Tringas's stairs in 2001
during one of their lessons together,
when Carl learned at least
as much about life
as he did about music.

Thanks to:

Sam White, Swamphouse Marina friend and
former probation worker; Lokken Millis;
Jennifer Brahair; Kate Ricker and
Rawleigh Tremain; and Ruth and
Julie Claire Uffelman

My children—Kate, Cecile, Eric Jon, and Carl

My husband, Eric

Assistant Chief Chip Simmons
of the Pensacola Police Department

And Françoise Bui,
my fabulous editor with
incredible instincts

GONE

James kicked off his flip-flops and dug his toes into the grass. "So, Connor, what was it like?"

"What was what like?" We sat side by side on an overgrown soccer field. The sun was warm on my bare arms and legs.

"That night. Must've been pretty trippy, huh? Pretty wild?"

I laced my fingers together. "I dunno."

"Course you do. It had to've been an incredible rush in spite of the outcome."

I gazed at the goal box across the field, plucking idly at the grass with my left hand.

He nudged me with his elbow. "Speak."

"Ryan said it was like walking on fire. Almost like being God."

"Was it?"

I paused, thinking, remembering. "No. It was sickening. I demeaned myself. I lost something I'll never get back."

"What?"

"I dunno exactly. Something without a name."

"Do you want it back—whatever it was?"

Again I hesitated. James and I seldom shared our most private selves. "Yes, I do."

I SPY

I watched my family from the other side of the glass. Because of the darkness outside and the bright lights within, they were unaware that I observed them. My father was helping Kathleen with her homework. When he gets involved, he always ends up straying off course and teaching stuff that has nothing to do with the assignment. It looked as though he was explaining cell division that night. I could see the drawing on the table.

My father is a chemist with the county's water department.

His job is to maintain water quality in the local reservoirs. Occasionally he has to close one if the contaminant level is too high. A typical scientist, he breaks everything down into the most basic elements. He probably dreams in molecular structure.

Kathleen appeared to be listening to Dad, but I'd seen that look in her eyes often enough to know that her mind was elsewhere. I remember the day she was born. I was seven, and I'd spent the previous few months placing my hands on my mother's belly to feel the baby kick and roll. Kathleen's a dreamy little eight-year-old—always off on some adventure in her imagination. She picks out the quiet shadows in the boldest landscape; hears the delicate grace notes in the wildest concerto.

Trent sat on the floor putting new bearings in his skateboard wheels. He held a screwdriver in his hand and had the cordless phone tucked under his chin. I knew by the expression on his face he was bored. Trent's in ninth grade—just over a year younger than I am. He probably knows more about me than anyone else. We've shared a room and clothes and toys since we were babies.

My older brother, James, who'll graduate from high school in May, stood at the counter eating a grilled cheese sandwich before dashing off to his job at the DramaRama movie theater. As usual, his energy level was so high it was nearly visible.

My mother was chopping vegetables at the counter. A skillet of olive oil, onions, and peppers sizzled on the stove. She was deep in thought, her eyes distant.

Mom teaches English composition at the local community college. She's a fanatic about proper grammar. When she watches the news, she corrects every minor infraction by the newscasters. When a commercial uses an incorrect tense or subject-verb agreement, she totally flips, saying if the advertisers can't get it right how can we expect to have an articulate society. Sometimes we use double negatives just to see her reaction. What really drives her nuts is something James started: saying *wit* for *with*.

One night when we were eating dinner, Mom said, "James, I need you to help me wit the dishes." She was so straight-faced about it that it took a couple of beats before we realized she was only playing him.

James winked and said, "Aw, Mom, I was gonna play video games *wit* Connor. Can't Trent help you *wit* them?"

My name is Connor Kaeden. I am not sure how that helps to define me. Probably not at all. That name was given to me at birth. I share it with a grandfather I never knew.

People liked Daniel. He had a comfortable way of moving and talking. He hardly ever got embarrassed. Even when he did something totally stupid, he'd just laugh and move on. Daniel was smart, too, even though he hardly ever made honor roll. He remembered stuff I would forget. Stuff like adventures we'd go on, but also the states and capitals we had to memorize in fourth grade, or the formula for photosynthesis, or the stats from the previous World Series.

Daniel and I were best friends ever since third grade, when we were on the same baseball team. I played shortstop with him behind me in center field. I was quick and agile. He could hit pretty good. Once Daniel caught a pop fly in center field and fired the ball to me at second. We made a double play and were heroes for a flash.

Our team didn't win a lot but Daniel and I had fun. We walked to practice together, talking as if we were big leaguers. In the dugout, we'd spit sunflower seeds at the NO PARKING sign we'd adopted as our target, or play endless rounds of rock paper scissors. On the field, we'd rag each other about strikeouts or fielding errors.

That was a long time ago. We don't play baseball anymore. Daniel doesn't play anything anymore.

I had agreed to meet Daniel and Ryan at Stingray's, a refurbished warehouse with a limited food menu and the mother lode of pinball machines, pool tables, and video games. We had no specific plans. Had I known Will Stanton was going to join us, I'd have ditched.

Will and Ryan were already there when I arrived. Will was leaning against a pole, leering at two girls playing Race Trak. One of them kept flashing him sultry smiles. The other ignored him completely.

Dressed in all black, Ryan was slouched casually in a chair near the front door. Even though it was nighttime and he was indoors, he was wearing sunglasses.

I wore jeans and my *Dark Side of the Moon* T-shirt with the trademark prism etched across the chest. "I see you borrowed your mommy's clothes again, Kaeden," said Will loudly. "I thought she told you to stay out of her closet."

I felt everyone's eyes on me, heard some giggles. I ogled Will's official Chicago Bulls jersey and expensive Nikes. "Funny, Stanton," I said. "Least I'm not an NBA wannabe."

Most kids from school didn't like Will much, but they had trouble excluding him. He had a warped sort of confidence. Even when the vibes suggested he should back off, he didn't. Oddly, he also had a magnetism that ensnared people in his power. Will required victims. If you weren't his target, you didn't dare intervene or he'd aim his barbs at you. I'd been on the receiving end of his assaults often enough to know that his venom was bitter and cruel.

I walked over to Ryan. "Where's Daniel?"

"Not here yet. Got any change?"

I pulled a handful of coins from my pocket. "A little."

He took four quarters. "Pay you back later." He fed twenty-five cents to the Double Diamond game machine. I heard bleeps and bells sound as the game selection panel flashed onto the screen.

"How can you play with sunglasses on?" I asked.

Ryan laughed. "Forgot they were there. No wonder I can't see." He pushed them onto his head.

"I didn't know Will was coming," I commented.

"Me either. Daniel set it up." His fingers danced on the touch screen. "There's a party at Chris's tonight."

"Chris Graham?"

"Chris Edelstein. Lives over on Hamilton." Ryan slipped another quarter into the slot. "Maybe we can stop by there."

"That'd be cool." I yanked my wallet from my pocket. "I'm getting a drink. Want one?"

"Dr Pepper. With no ice."

I walked to the counter and ordered. Someone slugged my upper arm.

"Connor," Daniel said, grinning. "Hey, man. Sorry I'm late. Mom wanted me to help her rearrange the living room furniture. Again."

"No problem. Want a soda?"

"No thanks."

The girl behind the counter handed me the drinks. "You didn't tell me Will was coming," I said flatly.

Daniel shrugged. "It was last-minute."

"Wish you'd warned me."

"Look, Connor, you just need to chill. Will's all right."

"He's a jerk," I said.

"Get over it." Daniel tugged at his ear. "Come on, we're taking off when Ryan's done."

"What's the plan?"

"Will's got something up his sleeve."

"Oh, great . . . one of Will's plans. What now?"

"He won't tell."

I walked back to the Double Diamond, where Ryan was finishing off the last quarter. "Here's your drink."

"Thanks." The machine flashed *Game Over*. Ryan stabbed a straw through the slit in the plastic lid.

"Let's go," called Daniel, and he, Ryan, and I met Will at the entrance to the arcade.

"Daniel's coming over?" my father asked. "Quick, hide the wrenches and screwdrivers."

We all laughed. The last time Daniel had visited, he'd been unable to resist the open toolbox and partially dismantled lawn mower Dad had left in the driveway when he ran to the hardware store for parts. "I'm really good at fixing things," Daniel had bragged.

"I dunno, Daniel, my dad doesn't like us to mess with his tools."

"I'll surprise him. The grass'll be mowed before he gets back." He picked up a screwdriver as he spoke, and, with the comparatively inexperienced and clumsy hands of a fourth grader, began detaching something from the main body of the engine.

"Daniel, better leave it alone."

"Relax. I do this kind of stuff all the time." A screw fell to the ground and bounced on the cement. "I'll get it later," he said as it rolled away.

"Dad likes to keep everything organized," I explained as I retrieved the screw. More and more tools and lawn mower parts littered the driveway.

"We have a Snapper," Daniel said. "You like this Murray?"

"I dunno. I don't mow the lawn. James does, or Dad or Mom."

"I do mine all the time."

"No you don't. Last time, your mom paid the kid across the street to do it."

"Only 'cause I was busy . . . hand me a wrench, will you?"

"Which one?"

"I don't care. I'm gonna use it to bust these two pieces apart." He was tugging at what I later learned were the carburetor and the gas tank.

"I don't think Dad does it that way."

He reached across me to grab a heavy wrench. Then he started bashing the piece. I could see little dents and scratches appear. At that point, my father pulled up. "What's going on here?" he asked with a less than pleased look on his face.

"I'm fixing it for you," Daniel said proudly.

"You seldom fix something by beating on it, Daniel." My father took the wrench from him.

Daniel looked up at Dad. "I'm not done yet."

"Oh, you're done, believe me," Dad answered. "Now go, both of you. Get away from here."

We wandered into the backyard. "I think your dad's mad at us," Daniel said as he hopped onto the tire swing.

"He's definitely mad," I admitted, wondering what sort

of punishment my father was lining up for me once Daniel
went home.

"I'd have fixed it, but I ran out of time."

"Maybe." I leaned against the trunk of our big oak.

"No, really. I'm mechanically inclined."

"Yeah? Compared to who?"

James called from the gate. "Connor, Dad wants you and
Daniel. Around front. Now."

Daniel and I exchanged looks. "Guess this is it," he said.

"Guess so."

We found Dad on the driveway, all his tools reorganized,
the lawn mower parts neatly lined up on a sheet of corrugated cardboard. "Yeah, Dad?" I asked in my most innocent
voice. "Need some help?"

"Funny boy," answered Dad dryly. "Sit down." He motioned to a spot on the pavement. The concrete was warm
from the sun. "First of all, if either of you ever touch my
tools again without permission, you'll pay dearly, understand?"

"Yessir," I said, and Daniel nodded.

"Second, you two are going to fix this machine."

Daniel grinned. "Really? Great."

"We don't know how," I protested.

"That's obvious," Dad replied.

We spent the afternoon putting the Murray back together. It took hours. My father patiently made us do the

bulk of the work, demonstrating at times, directing at others. Daniel enjoyed it, but I was quickly bored. "Dad, I'm getting mosquito bites," I complained in the hope that he'd dismiss us.

"Go put on long pants."

"Never mind."

A little later I tried again. "I haven't done my violin practice yet today."

"You can skip it."

By some miracle, when we finally yanked the pull starter, the Murray roared into action. "We did it," shouted Daniel, and he and I slapped palms. Dad groaned, but he was smiling at the same time.

"Go put the tools away. And when you're finished, bring me a cold beer." Dad pushed the lawn mower onto the grass to finish the chore he'd begun early that morning.

BEGINNING OF THE END

I followed Ryan, Daniel, and Will up the fire escape. We sat in a circle on the roof of Will's building. From some distant source, I heard scraps of music . . . was it Radiohead doing

"Karma Police"? I wasn't sure. The music was too far away, too faint, too clouded by the sounds of traffic, air conditioners, sirens, and people. I looked up into the sky, past the stars, to the very heart of the universe.

I'd known Ryan since elementary school. He started running with Daniel and me in fourth grade, when we rode our bikes to and from school together. We liked to see who could glide the longest without pedaling or race uphill fastest. Ryan was competitive, and even then, if he was losing, he wasn't above crashing into you to sabotage the game.

Ryan wasn't the sort to sit back and analyze a situation—he was the play-now-and-pay-later type. That probably explains why he got into trouble so often. It's also one of the things that made him fun.

Then, about halfway through middle school, Ryan got obsessed with his cool factor. His need for approval caused him to do obnoxious, stupid things—some hurtful to other people, some only to himself. Daniel and I liked him, though; we simply had to rein him in regularly.

Will was a different story. He made me uncomfortable from the start. The first time I saw him was in ninth grade. He walked into our algebra classroom as if he owned the world. He flung himself into a chair and stretched his feet out in the aisle, blocking the paths of a number of kids. His expression dared them to ask him to move. They didn't. Most turned away; a couple stepped over him.

Whenever possible, I avoided Will. He and Daniel had started palling around a few months ago, which sometimes made it difficult.

"Not much action up here," said Daniel, looking around the rooftop.

"We could go to Chris's," suggested Ryan. "He's having a party."

"Or back to Stingray's," I added.

"Don't worry, boys. This is the place to be," Will bragged. "Wait till you see what I've got."

TAGALONG

In my head, I replayed the conversation I'd had with Trent just before leaving the house. He'd flopped down on his bed across the room from me while I was getting ready to go out. "What are you doing tonight?" he asked.

"Meeting Daniel and Ryan at Stingray's. Not sure what's up. We'll decide when we get there."

"Can I come?"

"No."

"Why not?"

" 'Cause you can't."

"Daniel and Ryan won't mind. They like me."

"Trent, I let you come to the movies with us yesterday. And you went bowling with us last week. You can't come tonight."

He threw a pillow at my head. "So I stay home and play Monopoly with Kathleen? Thrill a minute."

I shoved my wallet into my back pocket. "Sucks for you, Trent. What are all your pals doing?"

"They're busy. Luke's out of town, Damon has some family thing going on, and Mike plays trumpet in the band so he's at the football game."

"Why don't you go?"

"A—no ride. B—no one to go with. C—I hate football games."

"Well, I'm outta here."

"Come on, Connor, let me come."

"No."

HEAT WAVE

James had an old blue Camaro that he bought from our cousin. It was battered and dented and the left front fender was black because he harvested it from a wrecked vehicle at the junkyard. Most of his pay from the DramaRama went into that car.

Trent and I loved riding in the Camaro. James always blasted the music and drove with the windows down. "The wind in your hair and the taste of asphalt on your tongue elevates the whole driving experience," he explained as he rounded a corner with the tires squealing.

"It's hot," complained Trent one sultry afternoon. "Turn on the AC."

"You can walk," James said with a grin as he tapped the brakes.

"Never mind." Trent reached over the seat to eject the CD.

James snatched his wrist. "Hands off, punk. I control the music in my car."

Trent glared at me when I laughed, but he withdrew his hand.

SCALDED

Will went to a battered chest of drawers someone had abandoned on the roof. He tipped it up and pulled something from beneath it. Something silver that gleamed in the moonlight. He brought it to us as if it was a prize and flashed it about carelessly, laughing. Then he held it out to me. I wish I had never touched it.

The gun.
I remember the feeling of it in my hand. The frigidness, the heaviness, the balance. I thought of my violin, warm and fragile. I thought of the power each promised. The hairs on the back of my neck awakened and rose with a chill.

The gun.
I remember the smell of it—acrid and chemical and metallic.

The gun.
I remember the sound of the cylinder as it spun before my eyes—a smooth seduction, a rhythmic cadence.
I passed the pistol to Ryan. My hand felt dirty, fouled, scorched.

FRAGMENT

It was the first week of summer vacation between seventh and eighth grades. Daniel and I got up early in the morning and walked to the freight yard, where we put pennies and nickels on the rails. I peeled an orange and handed half to Daniel while we waited for a train. The rising sun scattered fiery rays of crimson light all around us.

"I'm not going to Kuwait," Daniel said so quietly I barely heard him.

"Why not?" For months, he had been anticipating a trip to the Middle East, where his father worked in the oil industry. His parents had divorced when he was five, after which his father had wandered the globe in search of fossil fuels.

"Something to do with local unrest and terrorist threats," he mumbled. "Just another sorry excuse."

"Could be true. I always hear stuff like that on the news," I said.

"Right. Remember last year? It was an outbreak of bird flu. Or the time he was worried I'd get kidnapped and sold into slavery?" He picked up a handful of gravel and started throwing it, piece by piece, at the abandoned boxcar on a switch track. "I hate him. He's such a liar."

"You did meet him in Spain—"

"That was two Christmases ago, and only for a week. And I spent half the time babysitting his girlfriend's little brats."

"That would've pissed me off too."

Daniel fired a rock at the logo on the boxcar. It pinged against the steel surface and boomeranged onto the roadbed.

"I really thought it was going to work out this time. Looks like another summer with nothing to do."

"You can still go to the beach with us. Mom invited you, remember? We had fun last year."

"Maybe." He picked up another handful of gravel.

The vibrations shaking the earth told us that a train was coming long before we actually heard the song of wheels on tracks. Daniel sat on an old wooden crate and waved to the engineer. The train thundered past in front of us—a monster full of power and strength, but with very little freedom, trapped as it was on those steel rails. It was a freight train laden with promises for some faraway destination. I counted the cars . . . eighteen, nineteen, twenty . . . fifty-two, fifty-three, fifty-four . . . and finally, eighty-seven.

We jumped up as the last car passed, and collected our flattened money, which was still hot from the friction of the train's wheels. I spread out four coins on my palm: three pennies and a nickel. They were flat and lopsided, and the images once minted into their metallic souls were distorted and vague, but still visible. On one penny, Abe Lincoln's chin and nose were longer than ever in some kind of grotesque caricature. On the nickel, Monticello was curved on the horizon as if viewed through a concave lens.

I slipped the coins into my pocket and listened to them jingle as Daniel and I walked the rails. It was an ongoing competition with us. We would see who could keep his balance the longest. Usually it was me, but that morning Daniel's anger brought him focus. "I should walk all the way to California and never look back," he said.

FROZEN

"Where'd you get the gun?" Ryan asked, weighing it in his hand.

Will stretched out his arms and arched his back as if he was bored. "A guy," he answered after a noticeable pause.

"What guy?"

"Some geek at the Seventeenth Street flea market. No one *you'd* know."

"Yeah . . . right," Daniel cut in. "They don't sell guns at the flea market."

Will tossed his head and rolled his eyes. "Not out in the open. Jeez, you're dumb. But if you have the right connections . . ."

"Like you have connections," Ryan retorted. He sounded as if he didn't believe Will—as if he knew the truth was much tamer but Will was doing his tough-guy thing.

Will laughed mirthlessly—a sound like driving on an oyster-shell driveway. He fished a bullet from his shirt pocket and slipped it into one of the chambers. Then he twirled the cylinder. It hummed. "Russian roulette, anyone?"

Daniel laughed. "You're kidding, right?"

Ryan laughed too.

I must have been ridiculously naïve. "Russian roulette?" I asked.

They all laughed.

At me.

CHORDS

Stewart Anthony had the chair next to mine in orchestra class. He reminded me of Buddy Holly or a young Elvis Costello, with black-framed glasses and a tangle of curly dark hair falling across his forehead. He was a decent violinist, but on Fridays, when Mr. B gave us free music class, Stewart showed his true colors. He'd go to Mr. B's instrument closet and get one of the cheap plywood guitars issued by the school board. Once he'd commandeered a quiet corner, he'd tease that crummy six-string into some downright nice sounds. One afternoon I joined him.

"You're pretty good," I commented.

"Thanks. I fool around. You play guitar?" he asked.

"No."

He strummed the basic few chords all beginners learn.

"I could probably do those," I said.

"The top four strings are the same as on a violin. The bottom two are bass."

I went to the closet and took one of the guitars from the rack. It was scratched and horribly out of tune. "Yeah, not exactly a Martin, but it'll do," said Stewart when I strummed it. "It's different from holding a violin. This you caress." He positioned the instrument in my arms and proceeded to run me through the essentials.

On subsequent Fridays, Stewart and I usually sat together playing guitar. It was a nice change from the violin—probably like driving a powerboat when you're used to driving a car.

THE STAGE WAS SET, THE LIGHTS WENT OUT

Ryan explained Russian roulette to me. "You spin the cylinder without knowing which chamber holds the bullet. Then you point the barrel at your head and pull the trigger." He made it sound as obvious and easy as first-grade math.

"It's the ultimate gamble," Daniel added knowingly.

"But won't someone get shot?" I asked.

"Duh," said Will. "If the bullet is in the right chamber."

"Or the wrong chamber, if you get my meaning," Ryan said, laughing nervously.

"Sounds twisted to me," I said.

"That's 'cause you're such a little wimp," Will sneered. "If you had any balls you'd do it."

I looked at Daniel and Ryan. "Have you ever done it before?"

"Seen it on TV," said Ryan.

"And in movies," added Daniel.

"Seems kinda dumb," I said.

"It's a game, just a game, baby Connor," Will retorted scornfully. He raised the gun and it flashed in the moonlight. "There's only one round in it . . . the odds are in your favor."

"You're crazy," I whispered.

"Let's do it," Will said, his voice like rope burn.

My mind was a whirling cyclone. I could grab no images, words, or sounds. Everything was in a state of chaos. I felt myself losing control. I opened my mouth to protest but was mute. Did my face reveal my confusion? My fear? I reverted to a trick James taught me when I was in third grade and got the jitters before every baseball game. I started reciting the multiplication tables in my head. (One times one is one . . . one times two is two . . . one times three . . .) I waited for Ryan or Daniel to stop this insanity. They didn't. (Three times six is eighteen . . . three times seven is twenty-one . . .) Daniel coughed, turning his head toward the fire escape so that he didn't have to meet my eyes. (Five times nine is forty-five . . .) The wind sang through my hair, whispering a warning. Ryan squirmed and zipped his jacket. (Eight times nine is seventy-two . . . eight times ten is eighty . . . eight times eleven is eighty-eight . . .) I waited for Will to disarm the weapon and toss it aside. He didn't. (Nine times six is fifty-four . . . nine times seven is sixty-three . . .) I met his eyes and got so chilled that I lost my rhythm and couldn't remember what nine times eight equaled. Over and over I thought, nine times eight . . . nine times eight . . . nine times eight, but no answer came.

INVISIBLE LINES

My mother's brother, Pete, is an artist. He's my favorite uncle. I have all sorts of crazy and beautiful things he's made me over the years. "What do you think?" he asked one day after unveiling a new painting he'd brought to the house.

My mother and I stood before it. "A whole new tangent for you, Pete," she finally said. "Beautiful. The blues are exquisite."

"I'm particularly happy with the blues myself," he admitted.

"What's it called?" Mom asked.

"I'm not certain yet. Maybe *Jessica's Dream*. Jessica's the model."

I studied the canvas, following the paths of the brushstrokes and the energies of the colors. "It's lyrical," I said.

Uncle Pete looked at me. "You think so?"

"Yeah, it's like visual music," I explained, still gazing at the painting.

Uncle Pete looked pleased. "Visual music . . . I like that." He leaned against the wall and silently revisited his work.

Mom always says I remind her of Uncle Pete. Not the way I look—Uncle Pete is a big green-eyed man with thick red hair, and I'm a slender kid with brown hair and dark brown irises. Mom says I'm like Uncle Pete because we both do most of our talking with our eyes, not with our mouths.

Will spun the pistol around his index finger like a gunslinger in a bad cowboy movie. "Let's do it."

"Jeez, Will, cut it out," Daniel said nervously.

"Yeah. Let's get out of here," I said. "We could go to the reservoir."

"Or Chris's party," Ryan suggested urgently.

"Come on, boys. There's just one round. It'll be a rush. Besides, it's time for you innocents to lose your virginity."

"You've done it before?" asked Ryan.

"I've done everything before." Will thumbed the cylinder, setting it in motion. "What about it? Who's got the balls to stare death in the face? Are there any men here tonight, or just mamas' boys?" He pointed the gun at his ear. "I'll even go first—set the stage for you novices." I could see his hair grazing the barrel. I could hear the hushed sighs of the others as they watched. Tiny beads of sweat appeared on Will's forehead.

"You won't do it," Ryan whispered.

"Just watch me."

The muscles in Will's hand and fingers tensed as he squeezed the trigger. I heard him exhale. A metallic click stopped my heart. My bones felt like rubber bands. Daniel,

Will, and Ryan started to laugh. It looked, felt, and sounded as if we were underwater.

FAMILY PLAN

"I like it here," said Daniel, sinking onto the sofa. "There's always something happening. It must be great having siblings."

"I'd trade places with you in a heartbeat," said Trent. "Anything to get away from them." He sneered at James, Kathleen, and me.

"And we'd let you go with pleasure," said James, thumping Trent on the head.

"Hey now, don't pick on my surrogate brother." Daniel reached for the remote and surfed through the channels until he found *The Brady Bunch*. "All right. Let's watch," he said.

"Not that again," I groaned.

"Come on. This is the episode where Marcia and Greg both run for class president."

"Oh boy!" said James sarcastically. "I'd hate to miss it."

"Your family's just like this," Daniel said, gesturing

toward the TV screen. That certainly wasn't true—no family is like the ones on TV. Even the occasional dysfunctional TV families have nothing to do with real life.

POLAR OPPOSITES

Daniel and Will became friends in summer school last June, when they both had to retake biology. At first, Daniel would come around after class and tell me what a jerk Will was. He would describe the rude things Will did during class, and the way lots of the girls—even the sleazy ones—avoided Will.

At the same time all that was unfolding, Daniel's father let him down once again. He'd chartered a sailing yacht and promised to take Daniel on an Atlantic cruise from the Florida Keys to the Statue of Liberty. They planned to embark the Saturday after the two-week summer session ended. A week into classes, Daniel's father called to cancel, claiming an on-the-job emergency. Daniel was slammed. He raved and cursed. "Screw him!" he cried. "And screw his stupid toys." Then he smashed to toothpicks the model clipper ship his father had sent him.

By the end of the summer, Daniel was running with Will all the time. I felt left out, but usually chose not to join them. Will was brittle, with arctic eyes and an acid tongue. Only when I thought it through later could I find a good comeback for most of his jibes. I didn't like the way Daniel acted when he and Will were together. I couldn't see what Daniel found so appealing about Will.

UNDER PRESSURE

Will held the gun out to Ryan, who glanced uneasily at Daniel and me. "Spin it," Will hissed. His eyes looked hungry.

"I never said I'd play," Ryan protested.

"You can't *not* play now," Will said, shoving the gun into Ryan's hand.

"But I don't—"

"Do it." Will leaned toward Ryan with a sneer on his face. "What? You're too scared, little sissy girl."

Ryan closed his eyes for a moment. Then he squared his shoulders and straightened his spine. "Who are you calling a little sissy girl?" he muttered, clasping the gun. The weapon looked huge in his hand. He used his index finger to spin the cylinder and stared in morbid fascination as it reeled. Finally it clicked into place.

"Do it," Will commanded again. His eyes were flat and blank. "I did it. Now everyone has to take a turn." He cocked his shoulders back and jutted out his chin. "Do it."

I wanted to shout—to let Ryan know that it was okay not to participate. But something in Will's posture muted me.

Ryan took a deep breath and lifted the gun. He held it at an odd angle, pointed slightly up and out, but still at his head. I turned away. I did not want to watch. I did not want to be there.

The same metallic click as before shattered the silence.

Ryan sighed and threw the pistol at me. It landed in my lap. I didn't want to touch it.

"Go, Connor," Will chanted, and the others chimed in. I looked up. I felt trapped in a foreign place. "Go, Connor, go, Connor, go, Connor."

YELLOW CARD

Daniel, Ryan, and I were going to the vacant lot across the street from school to join a pickup game of soccer. "Hey, Connor, can I come?" asked Trent. He was still in eighth grade at the time—we were all in ninth.

I looked at my pals. Daniel nodded and Ryan shrugged. "Yeah, come on," I said.

The sky was boiling with dark clouds by the time we got to the lot, but that never stopped one of our soccer games. We paired off, Ryan and Daniel joining the skins team, and Trent and me on shirts. Within minutes, we were being pelted by large raindrops. A few of the guys left, but most remained on the field.

Trent and I had messed around with soccer balls since we could walk, so together, we made a great pair. We knew how to anticipate each other's moves. And that day luck must have been on our side, too, because nearly every play we executed came off polished and smooth. "Schooled you," laughed Trent as he once again danced past Ryan to score.

The next play Ryan fouled Trent hard from behind, knocking him off his feet. Shortly after that, Ryan slammed into Trent's chest with his shoulder. I heard my brother's lungs deflate with a dull *humph*.

The field was soon a muddy arena, and we were slipping and sliding every which way. Rain washed into our eyes and down our backs. It wasn't long before it became less of a soccer match and more of a brawl. A friendly sort of brawl, but with a few vengeful jabs slipped in here and there.

The rain stopped as Trent and I were walking home. "Ryan was getting a little rough there," Trent said, rubbing his shoulder.

"Yeah. He's like that, 'specially when he's on the losing team. He doesn't really mean anything by it."

"Look where he kicked me in the ribs." Trent lifted his shirt to reveal a pattern of scratches and darkening bruises.

"Ouch. Want me to call nine-one-one?"

"Very funny. I've got scars all over me—courtesy of Ryan."

"Ryan just gets carried away sometimes. You know that."

INTIMIDATION

"He's chicken," Will said scornfully. Then he tucked his hands into his armpits, flapping and squawking like a frightened hen. Ryan joined him. Daniel and I locked eyes. Then Daniel quickly looked away and softly said, "Just do it, Connor." I felt betrayed.

"It's your turn," said Ryan, suddenly bold.

I picked up the gun.

"Get with it," said Will.

"Spin it," Ryan whispered. "Now."

Following Ryan's example, I slid my finger across the cylinder and heard a gentle yet lethal hum as it twirled into position.

Oddly, my eighth-grade language arts teacher swept into my thoughts. I remembered him telling us about Damocles when we were studying Greek mythology and legend.

Damocles served as a courtier to King Dionysius of Syracuse, who was such a tyrant that he lived in fear for his life. When the king overheard Damocles envying the wealth and grandeur of his royal lifestyle, he invited the bold young man to trade places with him the following day. Come morning, Damocles lavished in luxury—being fed, pampered, and spoiled.

Damocles thought himself the happiest man alive until he looked up and saw a sword suspended directly over his head. The blade was dangling from the ceiling by a single horsehair. If the hair broke, Damocles' life would be over. He grew pale and nervous, and all pleasure he had enjoyed that day dissolved.

Damocles cried out to Dionysius for an explanation. The king told his courtier that although as ruler he indulged in many pleasures, he lived each moment in dread that he might lose his life to some intrigue. By suspending the sword over the young man's head, Dionysius gave Damocles a taste of his tenuous level of existence.

I always felt a secret connection to that story because

the bowstrings of a violin are made of horsehair. The horsehair bites into the violin strings with microscopic fangs.

With that gun in my hand, and the others looking on, urging me to do the unthinkable, I felt like Damocles. I glanced up, expecting to see a sword dangling above me.

REVOLVER

Spin it. It spins. It is hypnotic. It is like driving down the highway past acres of towering pines planted in evenly spaced rows. As you speed past, the trees dance before your eyes in rhythmic motion, mesmerizing you.

I spin it again. The chambers wheel before my eyes. They are black holes in space, sucking me deeper and deeper into their void.

EARTH-STARS

Early every spring, my mother raked away the weeds and dead plants outside the kitchen door and turned the soil. She always let me help. I liked the smell of the earth and the feel of it in my hands. When the ground was ready, we'd plant the seedlings she'd started in late winter and kept in the kitchen window until the weather warmed. She taught me how to pop the seedlings from the plastic flats, break up the root-balls, and cover them with soil. She compared planting seedlings to tucking her children into bed at night.

We grew the same things every year—zinnias, cosmos, larkspur, and my favorites—forget-me-nots, with their tiny blue star-shaped flowers. Mom told me that when I was about three, I called them earth-stars, which amused her. *Earth-stars* became our private name for those forget-me-nots—something only the two of us shared. We kept vases of earth-stars on the kitchen table all summer long.

James and Trent weren't interested in our garden. James wasn't patient enough to wait for the seeds to sprout, grow, bud, and finally blossom; if Mom let Trent in the garden, he only dug holes and tunnels for his toy trucks, uprooting her babies.

It wasn't until Kathleen was born that we found another gardening partner. Kathleen loved growing things. She'd celebrate every new leaf, each emerging bud. The insects we found in the garden also fascinated her. She'd scoop them up and let them crawl on her hand, never worried that she'd get bitten or stung.

DOUBLE DOG DARE

"Go, Connor, go, Connor," they chanted.

Ryan was pounding his hands on his knees in a primal drumbeat.

"Come on, wittle Connor," Will whined in baby talk.

Will thrived on ridicule. In algebra class last year, the kid who sat next to me was kind of nerdy. He was so skinny that his clothes didn't fit quite right, and he had a really crummy haircut. He was nice, though, and always helped me when I got confused. Will victimized that kid regularly. He made loud sarcastic comments about the boy's clothes, shoes, or voice, and the poor kid blushed bright red. I felt ashamed to be sitting there, crippled by my silence.

And that night, there on that rooftop, I was that kid. I looked at them all, one at a time. Their eyes and the lines of their jaws challenged me.

I raised the pistol to my head. My bones felt liquid.

"Put it in your mouth. Taste it, baby Connor," said Will.

I thought I might vomit.

I felt the cold fear of contact as I pressed the barrel to my temple. I closed my eyes and uttered a silent prayer at the same moment that I squeezed the trigger.

It took hours, days, years, eternity.

Nothing happened.

The slap of metal on metal echoed through my ears, my mind, my bowels.

GAS

We once had a dog named Argon. Dad named him when he was in grad school, where he did his thesis on inert gases. Argon was a mutt. Hairy and nondescript, but with the prettiest eyes and sweetest nature of any dog I've ever known.

When I was little, Argon and I would lie together before the fireplace. He let me use his body as my pillow and licked my face to wake me. We were brothers at heart.

I played with Argon all the time. Sometimes he was my faithful steed, sometimes a fire-breathing dragon, sometimes a rabid coyote. He easily fit into whatever game I had going. He followed me everywhere.

When I was eight, I came home from school one day and Argon wasn't there. My father took me to a mound in the backyard and told me that Argon had run out of the house after my brothers and I left for the bus stop that morning. "A car hit him, son," Dad said sadly. "He was old. Probably couldn't see well."

I wept. Dad sat in the grass beside the mound and held me in his arms.

At the time, I only nursed my own grief. But later, when I was a little older, I realized that my father must have also mourned Argon's death. Dad had known Argon even longer than he had known my mother.

CHICKEN LITTLE

What did I do with the gun? I don't know if I dropped it, or if I handed it to Daniel, or if one of the others took it from me. I wish I had never touched it. It was such a small thing, but it held such power.

When my eyes focused again, Daniel had the weapon pointed at his head. His terror was palpable. His eyes suddenly huge. His lips quivering. Will and Ryan clapped and chanted, "Bang, bang, Daniel. Bang, bang."

Daniel dropped his hand to his lap. "Don't say that. I won't do it if you keep saying that."

"Oh, Chicken Little, do it," sneered Will.

In one fluid motion, before I could look away, Daniel raised the gun to his head and pulled the trigger.

There was no explosion. No smell of gunpowder. No blood. Daniel threw the gun into the center of the circle, obviously glad to be rid of it. "Put it away," he said to Will.

BROTHERHOOD

James, who is almost eighteen, isn't at all like me. He's daring and wild. Nothing frightens him. He moves like a wildcat. He dresses in an offbeat way that gives him style but looks mainstream enough not to make him weird.

People are drawn to James, probably because his quiet laugh and challenging eyes promise mystery and excitement. Everyone is always surprised to find out that we're brothers. "You're so different . . . he's so . . . you're so . . . I guess you do have the same eyes . . . ," they say. I don't respond.

Trent, who's fourteen, runs with the skater crowd, dragging his skateboard with him everywhere he goes. He's fast and athletic. James and I have always known that Trent is the golden boy of the family. When we were younger, people always told Mom, "Your children are so sweet . . . and that Trent . . . he's the cutest, smartest little guy." Teachers allow Trent to get away with things that would get most students in trouble. Other kids want to be Trent's friend. Somehow he comes out on top of everything he attempts.

Me? I'm fifteen and trapped in the middle. Neither gutsy nor golden, just quiet, dependable, unobtrusive. Of course, that was before.

PSYCHOBOY

"How about idiot's roulette?" Will suggested, picking up the pistol. He sounded sinister, malicious. Or maybe that's only the way my memory paints it . . . in brushstrokes of evil and anger.

"Idiot's roulette?" Ryan asked, confused. "What's that?" I felt relieved that someone other than me was now claiming ignorance.

"Yeah, idiot's roulette. That's my new twist to Russian roulette." Will leaned forward. He was so close that I could see every tiny hair follicle, every pore. "Instead of pointing the gun at yourself, you point it at the guy next to you."

"You're crazy," snapped Daniel.

"I'm not doing that," I protested.

Will resumed the flapping and squawking like a chicken routine. "Connor's such a baby," he sneered. "Somebody give him a pacifier." He shifted the pistol to his other hand and repeatedly twirled the cylinder. Six, seven, eight times. He raised the gun to Daniel's head. "Bang, bang, you're dead," he said, icicles crashing from his laughter.

Daniel pushed Will's arm away, his face pale, his pupils dilated. "Forget it, Will," he said. "Put it back where you got it."

"Let's go to Chris's party," suggested Ryan. "He said lots of girls are going to be there."

"Yeah, let's do that," I agreed.

Will laughed and pointed the gun at Ryan. "Or you, Ryan? Do you want a little taste?" Ryan ducked his head away from the weapon.

Again Will pointed the pistol at Daniel. I didn't believe he would pull the trigger. I expected him to drop the gun and end the game, the avalanche, the nightmare.

I was drained of all energy. I wanted to be at home. I wanted to be anywhere but there. I glanced at Daniel. He was turning away from Will.

SNAP

That single horsehair suspending the sword of Damocles broke, and the sword plunged down on me.

ECHOES

I still can't get over how loud it was. That was my initial impression . . . that endless, eternal explosion. Would it never cease? It echoed through my bloodstream, through my bones. Then my senses were flooded with smells and colors and someone screaming. Maybe it was me. I squeezed my eyes shut but still I saw Will smiling on the rooftop. I saw him with a clarity sharper than broken glass. I was cold, cold, cold. . . .

The dragon king, Quicksilver, slept in the ruins of an ancient citadel. From behind a wall, I watched his chest rise and fall in 4/4 time. He twitched his tail. A cloud of dust rose around him.

I crept across the yard and nestled against the curve of his body. His scales were smooth and cool. He caressed me with his tail. His heartbeats sounded like the drums of a warrior. I snuggled deeper into his chest, stealing his warmth.

I slept for a long time. Dreamless sleep. When I awoke, the dragon king was gone. I sat abandoned in the courtyard with sand stuck to my cheek. The moon was high in the sky. I picked up a silver mirror lying in the dust and held it to my face. It was not my reflection I saw in the glass. What I saw was the face of the moon, pale and alone.

Cold steel cut into my wrists. Lightning flashed . . . or was it just the lights?

Someone's hand on top of my head. Pressure there. The door slammed. I couldn't focus my eyes, and my ears were pounding and Ryan was wailing and Will was covered in blood but he was smiling. How could he be smiling?

And where was Daniel? I didn't hear his voice. I couldn't see him. I was confused and frightened. I knew something unspeakable had happened, but I didn't know what it was. I only knew that it involved Daniel. Where was he?

FOUR ON THE FLOOR

James was teaching me to drive. I wasn't very good at it. He'd tell me to let the clutch out gently and gradually accelerate, but I didn't have the right touch. We'd either lurch forward wildly or stall out.

"You're going to burn out my clutch," he cried one day. We were at a stop sign on a hill, and every time I tried to advance we rolled backward or the engine died. As cars lined up behind us, I became even more inept.

"You do it," I said after about five attempts.

"No. I'm a passenger."

"James, the people behind us are getting mad." I felt panicky.

"So?" He fiddled with the radio dials.

"What if I roll into them?"

"Not a good plan. Now go."

I inhaled, let out the clutch, and pressed the accelerator at the same time. The Camaro smoothly rounded the hill. James dramatically brushed the back of his hand across his forehead. "It's about time. You can stroke the violin with such skill. Why can't you drive a car? Anyone can drive a car."

INTERROGATION

They questioned me but I couldn't hear them because of the music in my head, which was loud and angry, and I couldn't see them because of the colors flashing everywhere. I wanted to scream and weep and die but I was frozen in that chair, in that room, with those men and their badges and questions and strong coffee. I tried to speak but my language had changed, and even I did not know what I'd said when the words came spilling out. I saw my mother and father through the glass and knew that they were terrified.

I squeezed my eyes shut and tried to banish the confusion in my head. There were people, telephones, files, telephones, coffee, telephones, guns, telephones, guns, telephones, guns, telephones. . . .

SHATTERED

Quicksilver danced with the sun. It blazed. It burned into my skin. It burned into my dreams. It revealed what I had hidden away so carefully. I felt exposed.

The dragon brushed me with his tail. It was like silken slaps.

Then he came at me faster, tossing me about.

Large and fierce, he landed before me. He plucked a scale from his breastplate. I heard a tone, F sharp, as he tossed the scale into the dirt at my feet. I looked down. From the scale came tangled rays of color, stirring the air like angry snakes. They *were* angry snakes. They bared their fangs.

Slender tongues darted from their mouths. Along with their venom, they spit out my dreams, one by one. My dreams lay scattered before me in the dust. They were now dead things. Spoiled. Ruined.

AFTER

Will was charged with an open count of murder, which the state's attorney would probably up to first-degree. He would likely be tried as an adult. Apparently he'd been in trouble before, so he already had a record. He was also charged with a string of lesser offenses. It turned out that he had stolen the pistol from his neighbor. It didn't surprise me that his flea market story wasn't true. I thought of his endless tales of bravado, and the way he had always ridiculed the rest of us for our inexperience.

Ryan and I were charged as accessories to murder. The police tacked on as many other crimes as possible—things like improper exhibition of a firearm, reckless display, trespassing, possession of a weapon while engaged in a crime, gun possession, and possession of stolen property. The lawyer told my father that many of the charges would probably be dropped—that it was common for the law to tag on every plausible offense and let the state's attorney whittle them down later.

Dad kept talking about lawyers and court dates. He always seemed to be on the telephone. My mother studied me as if she suddenly found me frightening—as if I would recklessly or deliberately damage myself further. I think she imagined the other invisible lines I might cross and brooded over the ones I might already have crossed without her knowledge. James treated me as if I was three years old, and Trent wouldn't meet my eyes. Kathleen brought me little presents—homemade cards and pressed flowers and turtles sculpted from modeling clay.

People came to the house; strangers. Lawyers and cops and social workers and the minister from the Methodist church around the corner. I was required to sit at the table with them as they opened their briefcases and clicked their pens, but I didn't speak. I had nothing to say.

Uncle Pete came to see me. We sat outside near the forget-me-nots by the back steps. Uncle Pete didn't talk about lawyers or sins or stable environments. He told me to play my violin. And he picked a bouquet of earth-stars to take home to his wife.

My mother entered my room and sat at the foot of my bed. "Connor," she said.

I pretended to be asleep.

"Connor." She spoke a little more loudly.

I inhaled. "What?" I was facing the wall and didn't turn toward her.

"I just got off the phone with Daniel's mother."

I felt nauseated. Pulled my knees toward my body.

"She asked if you'd play the violin at Daniel's service."

"What? No."

"She said she'd understand if you refused, but Connor . . ."

"I can't do it." I closed my eyes.

"It would be a nice way of telling Daniel good-bye." Her voice was soft, a little tentative.

"I don't want to tell him good-bye," I muttered.

"I understand, but sometimes we have to do what we don't want to do."

"And sometimes we don't."

She paused. "Connor, your music is a gift. It might help you to share it." She put her hand on my back. "And help her, too." I wrapped my arms around myself. I could hear my mother breathing and knew she was searching for what to say. "She needs an answer tonight. They're planning the service now."

"I can't do it."

"Connor—"

"I. Can't. Do. It."

She sat there, still touching me. I wanted to pull away but thought it would offend her if I did. She finally spoke. "You're sure?"

I yearned to scream. To scream and scream and scream and ride the sound waves to some faraway place. Instead I took a breath and softly said, "I'm sure."

"I'd better go call her, then."

HEARTLESS

Daniel, Trent, and I were hanging out in the bedroom Trent and I shared. I was worried about the upcoming math test because I didn't quite grasp translating fractions into decimals and percents.

"Get your math book. I'll show you how it works," said Daniel.

"Okay." I opened my backpack, pulled out my sixth-grade text, and tossed it on the bed. A bright red envelope fell out.

Daniel grabbed it. "What's this?" he asked as he glanced at the front. " 'To Connor.' Who gave you a card? With girly writing?"

"Give it here," I said, trying to snatch it from him.

He twisted away and held it in the air as he extracted the card from the envelope. "Ooooh, a valentine! Look, Trent."

"Give it back."

Trent joined the fray. "Who's it from?"

Daniel opened the card, holding it just out of my grasp. "From Molly." He grinned. "You got a valentine from Molly? And an expensive one at that! From the birthday card department at the store, not the cheapie kind everyone gives out in elementary school."

"Give it here," I demanded, still grabbing at it. Daniel jumped onto the bed and waved the card and envelope over his head.

"Who's Molly?" asked Trent.

I yanked Daniel's arm, but he switched the valentine to his other hand. He started reading the poem written on the front of the card.

"A *valentine comes from the heart*
And is the perfect place to start . . ."

He opened the card to read the rest.

"*To tell you what I want to say;*
I like to see you every day."

"Well, ain't that sweet?" said Trent in a syrupy tone.

Daniel then read the inscription in a falsetto that sounded more like Mickey Mouse than any of the girls I knew. " 'Connor, you're really cool! Molly.' "

I could feel my face turning as red as the envelope. "It's not like I asked her for it," I defended myself as I jabbed at Daniel's arm. "And I didn't give her one."

"Connor's got a girlfriend," Trent sang.

Daniel waved the card in my face. " 'Connor, you're really cool.' Gee, Connor, Molly thinks you're really cool."

Every time I thought I'd caught the valentine, Daniel jerked it away. "Give it back," I demanded.

Daniel made juicy kissing sounds while Trent continued to sing.

"She sits next to me in science. She's not my girlfriend or anything," I protested.

They laughed hysterically. Trent was lying on his back kicking his feet in the air. Daniel leaped from the bed and began rolling on the floor, clutching his sides. I snatched the valentine, but Daniel didn't let go, so it ripped in half. That made the whole situation even funnier to the pair of them.

Daniel sniffed at the piece left in his hand. "I think she sprayed it with perfume. It smells all prissy."

"No it doesn't. And I was going to throw it away."

"Bet he sleeps with it under his pillow," Daniel said to Trent.

"Or next to his heart," Trent added.

"No I don't," I insisted as I managed to grab the other half of the valentine. I stomped from the room and ripped the evidence into tiny fragments before throwing it away. Then I went outside to the picnic table in the backyard to escape their taunts.

"You're not really mad, are you?" Daniel asked when he joined me a few minutes later.

"Molly's *not* my girlfriend."

"Hey, at least she's cute."

"She's not my girlfriend. I swear."

"Did you kiss her?"

"Yuck. No. She's *not* my girlfriend." I glared into his eyes. "You're just jealous because you didn't get a valentine. And if you tell anyone at school about this, you're dead meat."

"Your secret is safe with me." Daniel winked and picked up a soccer ball lying in the grass. "Come on." He kicked it toward me, and I kicked it back.

Trent told James about the card. The three of them ragged me about Molly for months. Trent even retrieved the scraps of valentine from the trash and attempted to piece them back together, but, as Trent isn't terribly patient, he gave up quickly. At least Daniel kept his word. He told no one.

DIRGE

Everyone in my family went to Daniel's memorial service. The chapel was packed. Daniel's mother was receiving mourners. Her face looked like ashes and her hands were empty. A man stood beside her with his arm around her waist. I wondered if he was Daniel's father, whom I'd never met. When we reached her, Daniel's mother hugged me so close I could smell her natural scent beneath the fragrance of her perfume. She didn't speak, but ran her fingers through my hair, her hand lingering there a moment. It was puzzling: I had been frightened of confronting her—had expected rage or indifference, not tenderness.

I saw Ryan with his parents. He was pale. His mother stared straight ahead, her shoulders rigid. His father repeatedly adjusted his necktie and checked his watch. Kids from school crowded into the building—many of them crying. People, young and old, turned to look at me, or pointed me out to those around them. They did the same thing to Ryan. Their eyes were invasive.

Will wasn't there. I knew he was out of jail—that his uncle had put up bail so that he'd be free until his court date—but I hadn't really expected to see him.

Ryan and I exchanged glances. He looked like a small animal trapped in a rapid current. I wondered if I appeared as scared and helpless. I sat between James and Kathleen and was grateful for the security of their presence. Kathleen squeezed my hand. Tears tried to slip from my eyes. I closed them and breathed shallow gulps of air. I reverted to that old trick of James's and recited multiplication tables in my head.

People got up to speak about Daniel. They told stories of who he was, and who he might have become. And I recited multiplication tables.

The minister read selections from the Old and New Testaments, and Daniel's cousin sang a solo while someone played piano. And I recited multiplication tables.

Finally it was over. People gathered in small groups talking softly and hugging each other. I saw Stewart, that kid from my orchestra class I jammed with on the guitar. I recalled that he and Daniel had played baseball together freshman year. He briefly met my eyes but I turned away without any acknowledgment. I didn't want to face him, so I escaped to our car. And I recited multiplication tables.

I found an island in an ocean made of glass. The sole crea-ture to visit me there was Quicksilver, the dragon king. At dusk, he was silent as he soared in circles above me. The only sound I heard was the music that occurred when the wind brushed his scales. It sounded like bamboo chimes hanging from the limb of a leafless tree.

Quicksilver was always magnificent. At first, I could only look at him—a bright jewel from heaven. His body was slender and sleek, glistening in the moonlight. His colors were sweeter, richer, sharper, deeper, softer, finer, fiercer, and subtler than anything I had ever imagined. They were the colors of light and darkness and rain. The colors of birth and death. The colors of pain. The colors of ecstasy. The colors of love and hatred.

At night, Quicksilver came close and whispered my se-cret name. Though I didn't understand his ancient reptilian language, he spoke in words that sounded like poetry. Occasionally, he urged me to fly away. I told him I could not fly, but he didn't believe me.

I could never predict how he would behave. Sometimes he was playful and tried to make me laugh. He tickled my neck with his whispers and sighs. Other times he was fierce and frightening.

He came to me offering trinkets and treasures from his lair. These were not the things I desired. What I needed was elusive, like cotton candy on your tongue. It was out of my reach, teasing, taunting. Lingering just beyond my vision. But this I did know—you could not touch it.

At dawn, the magnificent beast scratched my arms with his claws, leaving a calligraphy that I was unable to read. Then he flew up to the clouds, trailing a streak of shimmering light.

TREBLE CLEF

Mom and I went to a nice neighborhood with lots of old buildings and houses. The clouds in the sky were wispy streaks, as if someone had dragged a feather through splashes of white paint. We came to a brick town house with big terra-cotta pots of pink impatiens lining the steps. My mother held one of my hands, and in my other I held a violin. The instrument seemed huge then, but I soon outgrew that one and had to move up to a larger size. Mom rang the bell while I ran my fingers across the slick surface of the brass nameplate screwed into the heavy wooden door. I was six years old, and about to have my first violin lesson.

The man who came to the door was tall and silver-haired. His mustache looked like the clouds above, white and wispy. "Hello, Connor. I'm Mr. Danescu," he said. We followed him into his studio. He had to lower the music stand to suit my small stature. The things he showed me seem so simple now . . . how to rosin the bow, how to hold the instrument, how to stroke the strings.

He named the notes tangled in the five-line staff and the strings of the violin. I didn't think I would ever sort it all out. I was afraid that I would not be able to learn this new language written in letters, numbers, and symbols.

MIDNIGHT

When I wandered around the house in the darkness, James wasn't always there. His bed was empty. His car wasn't in the driveway. Maybe he always stalked the night but I'd been unaware, since I'd slept more soundly before.

After Daniel's shooting, I woke up not believing what I had done. Not believing how close I'd come to killing myself. Over and over, in my mind, I pulled the trigger and everything exploded in waves of black, crimson, and violet.

Then I squeezed my arms for reassurance that I really was flesh and bone and blood.

The gun kept snaking its way into my thoughts, turning my music into something discordant. It breathed. It was a parasite—sucking life and energy from those who touched it. I could hear the gun barking its laugh at all of us. Daring us. Sneering. The gun always gets its pound of flesh.

I tried to think about other things . . . music or my childhood or school stuff . . . but that vision invaded. It was much more powerful than anything I could conjure. It owned a part of me.

DOUBLE, DOUBLE, TOIL AND TROUBLE

I returned to school two days after Daniel's service. It was difficult. People I had known for years acted uncomfortable around me. I had more or less expected that.

What I hadn't expected was that people who had never before given me a second glance gravitated toward me. I felt their presence, heard their voices, but their words I ignored.

They acted as if I was mysterious. Or tragic. Like one of Shakespeare's doomed characters—Hamlet or Macbeth. It made me sick. I never wanted to be anyone's warped symbol.

Ryan sought me out in the parking lot after school my third day back. "People are freaking out," he said.

"I noticed."

"Half of them act like this whole thing is our fault."

"Well, it is, sort of."

Ryan's voice dropped so that I had to take a step closer to hear what he was saying. "You know what's weird, Connor? Up there on the roof, when I actually pulled the trigger, I thought I was the toughest, wildest kid anywhere. I thought I could walk on fire. I imagined telling people about it and how impressed they'd be. But it's not like that. Everyone keeps asking me what it proved and saying how stupid we were."

"It was stupid. We *were* stupid."

"But at the time it didn't feel like it."

"It did to me . . . which makes it that much worse." I met his eyes. "I only wanted to get out of there . . . away from the gun . . . away from Will." I kicked at the loose dirt on the pavement. "Where is Will?"

"They won't let him come back. He's going to one of those schools for at-risk kids till his trial."

"Good. I don't want to see him. It's bad enough as it is."

Ryan folded his arms across his chest. "I'm just pretending nothing happened. That's my strategy."

"How do you do that?" I asked, astonished.

"Like this." He breezed over to a couple of freshman girls and started chatting them up. I walked to James's Camaro, where he sat behind the wheel gunning the engine.

WHEN I LOOK THROUGH THE WINDOW

Mom quit reading the newspaper after that night on Will's roof. People wrote articles, editorials, and letters about what had happened, and she didn't want to let any more of that nightmare into her life.

My father, though, slammed those words on the table in front of me and demanded that I read them all. He wanted to make sure I understood what I had been involved in, how everything was shattered now.

Just before I tucked my violin beneath my jaw and raised the bow, I looked into the auditorium. My parents and brothers were seated not too far from the front. I felt so small standing there, center stage: a six-year-old playing in his first recital ever.

The other students were all gathered backstage, studying their sheet music, polishing their instruments, or arranging their clothing. Some clowned around, dealing as best they could with that odd combination of confidence and nerves. At recital, we all played solos with a piano accompanist. Those solos were much more frightening than my middle and high school orchestra concerts, where I sat with all the other string players—just one among the throng.

My piece was simple, lasting less than a minute. I'd practiced at home and at rehearsals. I'd run through it with Mr. Danescu countless times. But at home no one knew if my fingering was wrong or my C was a little sharp, and at rehearsals all the students supported each other. Here, I was completely on my own.

I felt all their eyes on me. Waiting. Watching. My mother smiled and my father flashed me a thumbs-up. James stuck out his tongue and then grinned. Trent had rolled the program into a tube and was viewing me through it like a pirate with a spyglass. I closed my eyes, inhaled, and stroked my first note. Then another and another, until I finally finished the short piece. It was such a challenge then but seems so very basic now.

Everyone clapped. When I walked backstage, Mr. Danescu congratulated me. The older students slapped my palms and told me I totally rocked.

Each year after that, the process was repeated. As I advanced, my pieces grew longer and more daring. But still, I never got over all those eyes, waiting, watching.

SLASH

My mother bent over Kathleen at the table. "You forgot the second step—addition. Try it again."

"I hate math."

"I know, but you have to learn it anyway."

"It's stupid."

"Oh, Kathleen, you use math all the time without even realizing it."

Suddenly Trent, who was across the room plugged into a

video game, spoke loudly. "Yeah, Kathleen. Like if there are six chambers in the cylinder of a gun and only one contains a bullet, what are the odds of getting shot?"

James, Mom, Kathleen, and I froze in stunned disbelief. Trent threw down the controller in his hand and glared at me from across the room. "Well, Connor, you oughta know—what with your personal expertise in that area."

I was too stung to respond.

James jumped from his chair, his eyes ablaze. "Is this your idea of a joke, Trent? 'Cause if it is, it's not funny at all." He grabbed the front of Trent's shirt and yanked him to his feet. "What's the matter with you, you sick little psychopath?" He shoved Trent, slamming him against the wall.

"Lay off me, James. I'm not the one you oughta be ragging. Connor's the one who—"

"Shut your slimy mouth. Connor's not sitting here making warped jokes in front of Mom and Kathleen. What's the matter with you?" James grabbed Trent beneath his chin, pushing him against the wall and forcing him to stand on tiptoes.

"James, stop!" my mother screamed. I turned at the sound of her voice. Kathleen sat beside her, crying quietly.

James let go of Trent, but not without shoving him first.

HOUDINI

With Dad and my lawyer—whose name I can never remember—I went to see the prosecutor. A clerk came into the office with bulging file folders. The attorneys pulled out photographs and asked questions. My father sat rigid and serious, talking in a businesslike manner, answering queries addressed to me because I couldn't push the words through my lips.

I remained numb until I felt Quicksilver's breath on my neck and heard him whisper my secret name. Then he sang a dragonsong in his beautiful, mysterious language and I fell from the prosecutor's office and onto my island in its ocean of glass.

STRINGS

I had not touched my violin since that night of echoes and death. Somehow it seemed corrupt to touch something so undefiled with my hands so stained.

I woke in the middle of the night. An abyss threatened

to swallow me. I walked into the family room, where my instrument leaned against our old upright piano. I opened the case, feeling the same apprehension that you feel when you look into the mirror after you have sinned. The instrument's finish burned fiery in the moonlight coming through the window. I took the bow from the case. My hands felt like traitors as I tightened and rosined the bowstrings—as if by pulling that trigger I had betrayed all the honest things my hands knew.

I picked up the violin and began to stroke its strings. The music was mournful and desperate and afraid. But I continued to play anyway, because my demons scattered at the sound. For the first time since Daniel's death, I could breathe a little bit.

OZ

"Sucks what happened to Daniel," said Stewart one Friday afternoon as we plucked those guitars from Mr. B's closet. "You must be going through some serious hell."

I glanced away from my instrument to look at him. I wondered if he was another one of those people seduced by trouble—who can't stand not being part of the drama. One look at him revealed genuine concern.

"Yeah." I strummed a C chord followed by a G. "I'm . . . well, I guess it's like I'm pedaling but not getting anywhere."

"Like one of those dreams where you run and your feet move but you're stuck in one place?"

"Exactly." I rested my arms on the guitar. "I lie in bed at night and it replays itself nonstop. I can't shut it off. And each time the same things happen. I keep thinking *if only this, if only that.*"

"It doesn't help to go there," he said. "To the land of if."

"Like the land of Oz?"

Stewart laughed quietly. "Without the ruby slippers for escape." He polished the surface of the battered guitar with a flannel cloth. It was a habit learned from maintaining his violin. But no amount of polishing could help that abused six-string.

SCARS VISIBLE

One hot summer night when we must have been around twelve, Daniel and I went to the reservoir with some other kids and raced our bicycles on the embankment. I remember the songs of the crickets filling the air; the stars reflected in the still water; the humidity grasping my skin with its breath.

There were some girls there too. I was showing off, thinking they were impressed. Looking back, I don't think they noticed me at all.

We raced around wildly, laughing and yelling. The smells of summer charged through my bloodstream—grass and heat and freedom. Daniel and I were flying in opposite directions, swooping nearer each other with every pass. Finally, the inevitable occurred, and we collided. My cheek split open and Daniel gashed his scalp. Blood ran into my mouth and down my face, staining my shirt and tasting of iron. We went to the hospital, where we each got stitched back together. Daniel's hair hid his injury, but my face looked raw and angry for a while.

OH BROTHER

I walked into the bedroom I'd shared with Trent since we were babies. He was sitting on the floor wrenching on a busted remote-control car. "Hey, Trent."

He didn't respond.

"Think you can get it to work?"

No answer.

"Trent, this is stupid."

Silence.

"What do you think you're proving?"

He started singing that old Nirvana song. "Just because you're paranoid . . . don't mean they're not after you . . ."

"Grow up, would you?" I fell onto my bed and grabbed the book I was assigned to read for English.

MENTOR

Mr. Danescu's town house always smelled the same—a curious combination of the rich herbs he cooked with and the lemon oil his housekeeper used to polish the furniture. I hadn't been there in weeks, but Mom insisted that it was time, so I took my violin and sheet music and found myself once again in his studio—afraid of his recriminations and disappointment—afraid of what I might, or might not, see in his eyes.

As I tightened the bowstrings, he said, "Welcome back, Connor. Let's see . . . we were working on that Vivaldi, weren't we?" He sat at his piano and struck the notes I needed to hear to tune my instrument. I was flooded with a sense of relief. He showed no curiosity; passed no judgment. He treated me just as before.

I stumbled through the piece the first time, and he raised his eyebrow. "Breathe," he demanded. "Live the music."

So I tried again, and a few measures into the second run-through, the music took me in its arms and carried me away.

TRICK OR TREAT

I looked at the tattered wad of plastic and fabric in my hands, then glared across the kitchen at Argon, who wagged his tail. "He ate it," I sobbed.

"Actually, he only gnawed on it," said James, who, at eight and a half, thought he knew absolutely everything.

"It's ruined."

"Wear something else," said my father.

"I don't have another costume," I whined.

"Well now, Connor, anything can be a costume," my father said, wiping away my tears. "Even this." He grabbed the big bag of Purina Dog Chow from the cabinet.

"That's dog food," Trent said, adjusting his plastic fangs.

"Right you are!" Dad dumped the remaining beefy chunks into a grocery bag. Then he took a pair of scissors and cut holes for my head and arms. "Try it on."

"But I was gonna be Spider-Man."

"Argon got the best of Spider-Man, so we improvise. Try it on." I lifted my arms and he slipped it over my head. It smelled like the dog food aisle at the grocery store. "Now for the finishing touch." He reached for the Milk-Bone dog biscuits on top of the refrigerator and withdrew several bones. "Sir Galahad, get my drill." He was talking to James, who was already fully outfitted as a knight in shining plastic armor. When James returned, Dad bored holes in the bones, strung them on a shoelace, and hung a Milk-Bone necklace around my neck. "Go look in the mirror."

"I want that costume," Trent complained. "I don't wanna be a Martian vampire anymore."

"No way. Dad made this costume for me," I protested.

My mother laughed. "Well, at least he'll be popular with the neighborhood canines." She drew whiskers on my face with her eyeliner.

I smiled and wagged my tail—a frayed piece of rope hanging out from under my paper costume. Argon circled me, hungrily sniffing at my curious attire.

TUESDAY THE FIFTEENTH

Sometimes something is just broken. It can't be fixed with new spark plugs or superglue or galvanized screws. Sure—you can try to mask its brokenness with paint or duct tape or veneer, but inside, the brokenness remains. So really, all you can do is destroy it completely if its brokenness offends you—or simply love it in spite of its brokenness. But it can't be fixed and it is useless to try.

SUNDAY NIGHT

"Sit down, Connor," said my father. He and Mom sat at the kitchen table.

"Yessir?" I slid into an empty chair.

"Tomorrow's your final court appearance. You remember that, don't you?"

"Yes." Like I could have forgotten.

"Are you ready?"

"Yes."

"You know how to dress and act?"

"Dad, I'm not a moron."

He got *that* look in his eye. "We could argue that one, but I don't have the time or the energy." He turned matter-of-fact again. "They'll present your plea agreement. The terms have already been set—all you have to do is tell what happened and sign some papers. And whatever else the judge or lawyers say."

"Okay."

"Don't do anything stupid. There's a lot riding on this."

"Dad, I'm not going to do anything stupid."

He looked at me as if I didn't have enough sense to know what qualified as stupid.

My mother spoke. "Your white shirt and navy pants are hanging behind your door. I ironed them earlier."

"Thanks, Mom."

"I won't be there. I can't miss class again. It's the last week before the final and my students will be loaded with questions and concerns."

"It's okay, Mom." Actually, I was glad she wasn't coming. It was hard enough having it all laid out before my father.

Quicksilver sat on the stairs, his eyes as bright as emeralds. I took my violin from its case. The strings called out to me in the key of A minor. I picked up the bow and it danced across the instrument.

The music fell to the floor, shattering like glass. Quicksilver exhaled and blew away the shards. Moonlight coming through the window kissed his luminous dragon's scales. They turned into moths, fluttering upward and clustering against the bare lightbulb.

The violin wept tears of blue glass. They flowed out the door and saturated the ground. Where the tears bled into the earth, cerulean forget-me-nots climbed toward the stars.

PLATEAU

Daniel and I were walking home after a game of basketball at the park a few days before Daniel's death. "Will's not a very good shot," Daniel commented.

"He's clumsy."

Daniel laughed. "It makes him mad, too. He thinks he's such a badass, but he was lost out on the court."

"Will's a loser."

"He's okay."

"There's something off about him, Daniel. Something . . . I don't know exactly. But he chills me."

Daniel laughed. "That's ridiculous."

"You and Will—you're real tight, huh?" I asked.

"Sometimes."

"So what do you like about him?"

Daniel paused. "I don't know. Nothing intimidates him, and he doesn't take anything off anyone."

"Those are his good qualities?"

Daniel stopped walking and turned to face me. "It's weird, Connor, because when I think about it, I don't really *like* him all that much. He doesn't care what I think or how I feel. He just appears, makes plans, takes control, and there I am. Tangled up in his adventures. Thinking it's great at the time, but regretting it later. He's not such good company. I guess you're sorta right about him—he's got a mean streak."

"So don't hang out with him."

"I'm not going to anymore."

I believe Daniel truly wanted to break away from Will but couldn't. I always thought of Daniel as the stronger of the two of us. Now I remember how much power he gave Will, and I'm not so sure.

I had to go to a probation officer named Mr. Driver. That's what the judge said when he let me cop a plea. James drove me to a cluster of government buildings east of downtown in his old Camaro. "You scared?" He checked the rearview mirror. The car's engine made a thunderous drone as we raced through the streets.

"Yeah, sorta."

"Whadda you have to do there?"

"I don't know. He goes over my plea agreement and makes sure I'm doing what I should. Kinda like a babysitter for messed-up kids." I gazed out the window at the clouds.

"Want me to go in with you?" He pulled into an empty parking space.

I *did* want him to come—to guide me through this frightening new nightmare—but I also knew that I had to do it on my own. In some unwritten way, that was part of the test, for me at least. "No. I'll be all right."

"I'll be across the street at that diner."

I went into the Juvenile Justice Center—an unloved, generic piece of architecture on a worn-out street. I finally found the right floor, the right corridor, and the right little cubicle with a faded sign saying LAYTON DRIVER next to the entrance. There were no windows in Mr. Driver's office, just battered gray file cabinets and old wooden furniture. The dead plant in the corner had probably run out of carbon dioxide.

I stood there, unsure. A man typing on a computer sensed my presence. He looked up, then at his day planner, then back at me. "Connor?" he asked.

"Yessir?"

He checked his watch. "You're on time . . . that's good. Come in . . . sit down. I'm Layton Driver. Your probation officer." He reached across his desk to shake my hand. "I met your parents yesterday."

"Yessir, they told me about it."

"They're concerned about you, to put it mildly."

I hung my head, not wanting to meet his gaze. I knew how badly my parents had been burned by all that had happened.

He riffled through the debris littering his desk. He came up with a file folder labeled KAEDEN, CONNOR. When he opened it, I saw several documents clipped together, with lots of blanks begging to be filled in. "Let's get your paperwork complete. Let's see . . . you're fifteen . . . a sophomore?"

"Yessir."

"I'm looking at your plea agreement. Are you seeing a counselor or psychologist?"

"Not yet. My appointment's the twenty-second."

"With who?"

"Dr. Mitchell."

He made a note. "Make sure you don't miss it. . . . Community service?"

"I'm working at the cultural center. Playing violin for receptions and art openings, stuff like that. I've gone once."

"How'd that go?"

"Fine."

"Don't forget your documentation. Your time sheet needs to be signed every time."

"Yessir."

He looked back at the plea agreement. "What about the essay the judge wants . . . five thousand words on gun safety?"

"I'm working on it."

"Let me read it before you turn it in. . . . Fines and court costs?"

"My dad paid them. I have to pay him back."

"How are you going to do that? Do you have a job?"

"No. Not many people will hire a fifteen-year-old. I mow lawns and stuff."

Mr. Driver paused and looked at me for a moment. Then he wrote something on a Post-it note. "Go see this guy. Elwood Manulet. He's a friend of mine. Owns a hardware store."

I folded the pale yellow tag and put it in my pocket. "Thanks."

"You know you can't associate with Ryan or Will anymore. You understand that?"

"Yes."

"And if you break probation, your plea agreement is voided? Do you understand that?"

"Yes."

"I mean business, Connor. There's no fuzzy area. If you blow it, you blow it."

"Yessir. I don't run with Ryan anymore, and I never ran with Will anyway."

"There'll be random drug testing."

"I know."

"And I'm required to do home visits, check in at your school—anytime, day or night."

"My father told me."

I watched Mr. Driver make notes in my file. He must have been about forty but he had an ancient quality about him. His skin was pasty and his hair was thin and his voice held a slight tremor. He'd seen his share of trouble. I could feel that when I looked into his eyes. He'd seen other things too, but I wasn't sure what things.

"Yo, Mr. Driver, 'sup?" I turned to see a big guy with really bad teeth standing in the entrance.

"Hello, Arnold," said Mr. Driver.

"Not Arnold, Spike. How many times I gotta tell you that?"

"That's all for today, Connor. Come on in, Arnold."

"My name's Spike," the guy repeated. He snarled at me as we passed each other. He smelled of garlic and cigarettes.

I sat in the window and watched the rain scratch the glass. My music theory work sheet lay on the table in front of me, but I wasn't focused on it. Instead I was thinking about Daniel; about that night.

I remembered Daniel turning from Will; the gun in Will's hand; the concussion of bloodthirsty noise; the horrible jolt when the bullet made contact with Daniel's skull, ripping the world wide open; the wasted dreams as Daniel lay unmoving on the roof; the stars refusing to weep for him.

And Will shoving the gun into Daniel's pocket and smiling and Ryan screaming and crying and Daniel not moving or making a sound. But here's the strange thing: I don't remember being there. My own presence eludes me in these flashbacks. Where was I and what was I doing?

Sitting there listening to the rain, I realized how angry I was with Daniel. If he hadn't invited Will that night, none of it would have happened. How was it that I was able to see through Will, and Daniel couldn't? If he'd been more perceptive, everything would have been different.

I hated Will. It was a hatred with a razor's edge. I had a mental freeze-frame of him splattered with Daniel's blood on the roof. I'll never forget his smile—so full of lies and so triumphant. I never thought I could truly hate anyone, but I hated Will.

I wanted to talk to Daniel, to make him laugh. To see him tug on his earlobe when he didn't know what to say.

"Well?" my mother asked, jarring me back to reality. She was standing at the table.

"What?"

"How'd your session with Mr. Driver go?"

"Fine."

"Do you like him?"

I turned away from the rain and back to my music theory. "Seems okay."

She waited, but I wasn't sure what for. She cleared her throat. "What did he say?"

"Nothing."

"Connor, I'm tired of being answered in monosyllables. This is important to me, and ought to be to you, too." She sounded vaguely wounded.

"He just went over my plea agreement. Wants to see my essay."

"Have you finished it?"

"Not yet. I've done some."

"I want it finished by Monday. That gives you the weekend."

I looked up at her. "But, Mom, the judge doesn't need it until—"

"I want to see it by Monday. I'll proofread it before you turn it in."

"I don't think the judge cares about proper grammar and spelling."

"I care."

"Yes, ma'am."

ACID

I was in the school library, not to do research or read, but to escape the social scene in the cafeteria. I just wasn't into it. I randomly slid a book from the shelf. It was about masks from all around the world. I idly paged through it, biding my time until the bell rang.

"Hey, man." Stewart slid into the chair across from me. "Whatcha doin'?"

"Nothing really." I turned the page, wishing he would go away. The fluorescent lights cast a glare on the glossy paper.

"I bought an electric guitar at a yard sale this weekend. It's a cheap one. Might sound better with a new set of strings."

"That's cool," I muttered, not looking at him.

"Need to get an amp now."

"Oh."

He grabbed a book from the rack behind him and flipped it open. I caught a glimpse of black-and-white diagrams of some medieval machine. Stewart turned page after page. Finally he said, "I heard on the news that Will's being charged as an adult. Freaky, huh? First-degree murder and he's only sixteen."

I studied a page of two-faced Mexican masks and said nothing.

"I knew you ran with Daniel and Ryan, but I didn't realize you and Will were friends."

I looked up. There must have been fire in my eyes because Stewart pulled back a little. "Will and I were never friends," I said. "Never."

"Sorry. I just thought . . . since the four of you were all together . . . sorry."

I looked back at the book. "It's okay." I traced the spiraling horn on a brightly painted mask with my fingertip. Then I glared up at Stewart. "Is that what people think? That I liked Will? That I considered him a friend?"

"I dunno. Probably some people do."

I clenched my fists on the tabletop. "Even before he . . . did what he did . . . Will and I weren't friends. Daniel and Ryan, yes, but never Will. Not for the briefest moment."

I sat on the steps looking at the stars. The hinges of the front door squeaked. I turned to see James walk out and quietly pull it shut. He startled for a second when he saw me, then said, "What are you doing out here? It's after one."

"Nothing. Couldn't sleep. What are you doing?"

He sat beside me. "Nothing. I'm restless. Thought I'd go for a ride."

"Where to?"

"Wherever."

"Can I come?"

He paused. "Yeah . . . I guess. Come on."

I followed him to his car. "Do I need shoes?" I asked when the dew on the grass chilled my bare feet.

"Naw. You're fine."

I felt a rush of fear and freedom. I knew that I was skating the edge by doing this—that if Dad found out I'd snuck out with James in the dead of night, he'd be furious. And I knew that if the cops stopped us, I'd be out after curfew—breaking probation. Still, something in me needed this. Reveled in it.

James slipped the key into the ignition and turned it. The engine purred. "You ready to roar, Connor?" I looked at

James—at the sparks in his eyes and the iron in his smile, but I said nothing. "So talk—it won't cost you anything."

I laughed. I was feeling jazzed. We drove along at a sedate pace, observing traffic lights and stop signs. "You're a regular speed demon. Jeez, you're driving like Mom."

James grinned and said, "Patience."

We cruised to the tangle of cloverleafs that tied the highways together. James pulled off on a service road and idled beneath an overpass next to some other cars. There were people milling about and music blasting from someone's sound system.

"Why are we stopping here?" I asked.

"You're not scared, are you, little brother?"

"Me? No."

He winked. "Well, maybe you should be."

A tall Latino guy walked up to the driver's-side window. "Hey, man. 'Bout time you got here."

"Hey, Luis. Ready to get blasted off the map?"

"In your dreams, Lightning. In your dreams . . . who's that riding shotgun?" He peered into the car.

"My brother. He's navigating tonight."

Luis laughed. "Since when do you need a navigator, *hombre?*"

"Since he wanted to tag along. You ready?"

"Just about." Luis walked over to a red Mustang.

"Lightning?" I asked James.

He grinned. "I don't let it go to my head. Buckle up."

James and Luis pulled onto the service road and some other guys gathered at the corner. James revved his engine. Luis flashed him a smile and revved back at him. A blond girl waved a scarf and James jammed the accelerator. We lurched forward. Luis in the Mustang roared beside us. James's face was intense and his eyes focused. The engine screamed so loudly I could barely hear the radio.

I felt a rush of panic. "James! Slow down."

He grunted. It was something between a laugh and a snarl. "Not a chance."

Luis whirred past us and James cursed. "Don't break my concentration," he growled. The cement pylons supporting the interstate streaked past. We were moving too fast for me to count them. Then we took the lead. My heart was pounding, my blood pulsing in my ears. I anchored my feet against the dashboard.

James crossed the finish line half a car length ahead of Luis and let out a cheer. He braked, made a U-turn, and coasted to the place beneath the overpass where we'd first parked. Luis pulled up next to the Camaro and he and James jumped from their vehicles. Other people gathered around. "Nice ride, *amigo*," said Luis, clasping hands with James.

"Told you you'd eat my dust," James said, and Luis laughed. I watched from my place in the front seat, my brow cold with sweat.

We headed home an hour and a half later, after James

raced once more and we watched some other guys speed down the service road. "You do this a lot?" I asked.

"Often enough."

"Jeez, James, you're crazy. You must've been going over a hundred."

"Great head trip, wasn't it?" he responded.

"Weren't you scared?"

"More like exhilarated. You felt it too, didn't you?"

"Yeah," I said, but I wasn't sure. It had been an intense adrenaline rush, but frightening, too.

MULTIMEDIA

Last year, Daniel and I ditched school one day and wandered the streets around the university. We watched people doing what people do. Some strolled along casually. Others rushed to class, shuffling through their bags. Students and professors, or at least we thought they were professors, bought sandwiches from the deli at the corner. Girls flirted with boys. People passed footballs and sailed Frisbees and juggled soccer balls. Daniel and I laughed and talked about what we would do when we were older; how cool we would be when the girls flirted with us.

We sat on the steps of the library and made up stories about the people entering and leaving. We guessed what books they were looking for. The heavy blond girl in the frilly shirt wanted steamy paperback romances. The guy with the long brown ponytail wanted a vegetarian cookbook and some travel guides about backpacking in Europe. The two silver-haired ladies in silk dresses were interested in flower-arranging manuals. The couple dressed in black wanted a video of *Romeo and Juliet*. We thought we had figured it all out.

And now here I am, wishing I could go to the library to get the answers I'm seeking. I wish life was that organized. Then I could type my subject into the card catalog, and the screen would flash up the many sources I could consult to fix my life . . . to make my world sane . . . to turn back the clock . . . to make it unhappen.

BIOGRAPHY

I sifted through the newspaper articles in Dad's file folder. He'd shown them to me before, but I'd been so foggy then that I'd forgotten most of what they said. The headlines were like slaps—BOY DEAD FOLLOWING GUNPLAY; STOLEN GUN SPURS THREE ARRESTS, ONE DEATH; TEENAGER MURDERED ON ROOFTOP; SCHOOLMATES STUNNED BY SHOOTING.

I came to an article about Will. He was the youngest of three boys. The eldest worked in a transmission shop in Pennsylvania, and the middle one had left town at seventeen and hadn't been heard from since. His mother worked at the DMV. His father flitted from job to job and was seldom around. Will had been trouble since preschool. Some of his former neighbors and teachers were quoted saying they'd always known he'd come to no good. I wondered how he felt when he read those statements. Was he offended, indifferent, or did he laugh? Was he, like me, struggling to make sense of things?

W-2

I ironed my white button-up shirt and put on my newest pair of jeans. "Hey, James, this look okay? I'm applying for a job."

He looked me over. "Where?"

"Manulet's Hardware."

"Yeah, you look all right. Just act confident."

"I'm a little nervous."

"That's normal. Fake it. Good luck."

"Thanks. See you."

I rode my bike the mile and a half to Manulet's Hardware. It was one of the few independent hardware stores still around. It smelled like fertilizer and earth, with an undertone of axle grease. I walked up to the counter and stood to the side while two men discussed which type of air compressor was preferable. A tall, broad-shouldered man glanced at me. He seemed familiar but I couldn't decide exactly why. "Can I help you?"

"Yessir. I'm looking for Mr. Manulet."

"That's me."

"I'm Connor Kaeden. My . . . um . . . my . . . Mr. Driver suggested I come see you. I'm looking for a job."

"Catch you later, Elwood," said the other man. "Let me know when that gasket comes in." He retrieved a package from the countertop and left.

Mr. Manulet folded his arms and looked me over. There was something playful in his attitude. Suddenly I realized that he reminded me of Travis Tritt, Daniel's favorite country singer. Daniel and his mother loved the country music scene. "Layton sent you, huh?" He chuckled. "I wonder if he's put in his sweet peas yet."

I shrugged, unsure how to respond.

"He didn't tell you he grows sweet peas, did he?"

"No, sir."

"So, Connor, you want a job. What are you qualified to do?"

"I'm a hard worker. I'll do anything."

"Guess you've been in some trouble, eh, if Layton sent you."

I balked for a second, wondering what to say. I opted for honesty. "Yessir. I'm on probation."

He studied my face. "You get in trouble for thieving?"

"No, sir. Something else."

"I see. If I hired you, would you be an asset to my business?"

"Yessir."

"What kind of experience do you have?"

"Um . . . well, I know how to use tools and fix stuff. And I help my mother in the garden."

"Guess that's as good as most guys starting out. You're not a weakling, are you?"

"No, sir."

He laughed. "I was kidding. I can see you're strong enough for the work. I could use a fellow in the garden center. I can only pay minimum wage."

"That's okay."

"And you'll have to work weekends. That's my busiest time because all the recreational gardeners come in then."

"I wouldn't mind working weekends."

"You'll need to fill out some paperwork. Janice will set you up."

An older lady in the stuffy office at the back of the store handed me some papers. I filled out an application and the necessary tax form while she photocopied my learner's permit and Social Security card. When I was finished, Mr. Manulet was standing at a rack unpacking a shipment of hacksaw blades. "I'm all done," I told him.

"Great. Be here Saturday morning at seven. Wear your old jeans. George will give you one of our T-shirts."

"Thank you, Mr. Manulet. I'll be here."

"Fine." He shook my hand. "And it's Elwood, got it?"

"Yessir."

"See you Saturday."

"Thank you, Mr. . . . um . . . thanks, Elwood."

"Hey, James. I got it," I said when I walked into the house.

"The job? Awesome."

"What job?" asked my father, looking up from the newspaper. "Where?"

"At Manulet's Hardware. So I'll be able to pay you back faster."

Dad folded the newspaper and laid it across his knees. "You sure you can handle a job at this point? I can be patient about the money."

"It was Mr. Driver's idea, Dad. He's the one who told me to apply. He's friends with the owner."

My father thought about it for a minute. "It might work out. The responsibility could do you good."

IN TUNE

Stewart opened his violin case. "I didn't practice that new piece at all. I'm toast."

"Wing it," I suggested.

"Mr. B will know. He's like Superman—he has X-ray vision and otherworldly powers."

I laughed. "It's not difficult. Run through it before he starts class."

He placed the music on the stand and glanced over it. "Nah. I'm not in the mood. I'll just suffer the consequences." He began tuning his instrument. "Flat," he said when he plucked the D string. "I've hardly touched my violin all week."

"About all I do these days *is* practice."

"Guess it keeps your mind off things . . . ," he said.

I tightened my bowstrings. "Sometimes. It comes and

goes. I still can't believe what happened. It's weird, Stewart, but in my mind, I wasn't really there. It was Will and Ryan and Daniel, but the other guy—he was someone I've never known."

"What do you mean?" Stewart looked confused.

"It's freaky. Like some warped head game. Sometimes I struggle to remember who that fourth kid was."

"Maybe that's because you're someone else now."

I dragged my bow across the strings. "Yeah? Who?"

Stewart didn't answer. Instead, he turned the tuning peg and plucked the A string. "Sounds good." He raised his instrument to his throat and stroked it. "D's still off." He fiddled with the tuning pegs some more, but when he bowed it, it was sharp.

"Give it here," I said.

He spoke as I adjusted his violin. "I'm going to watch the symphony practice after school. Mr. B gives extra credit for attending. I need all the extra credit I can get. Totally botched that theory test. Didn't study." He took his violin. "Wanna come?"

"Can't," I said. "I've got an appointment." But that wasn't true.

MANUAL LABOR

I woke up early, got dressed in frayed jeans and an old T-shirt, and wolfed down a couple of bowls of Cheerios. I was putting the milk away when my father came in. "First day of work?" he asked as he started measuring coffee into a paper filter.

"Yeah."

"It's early. What time do you punch in?"

"Seven."

"Need a lift?"

"No thanks. I'm riding my bike."

When I got to Manulet's, no one else was there yet. I sat on the stack of forty-pound bags of fertilizer piled on the cement landing in front of the building. Someone pulled up in a rusty truck. "You the new kid?" he asked. He was in his twenties and built like a refrigerator.

"Yes." I stood up and brushed off my jeans. "I'm Connor."

"I'm George. Warehouse manager. Come around back to the employee entrance." He slipped a key into the door and I followed him inside. He showed me how to punch in on the terminal next to the back door. Then he gave me a brief tour of the store. It was a huge building with a lumberyard off to one side and a lawn-and-garden pavilion on the other.

I put my shirt in the locker he assigned and pulled a black and white Manulet's Hardware T-shirt over my head. The logo—wrenches crossed behind a flywheel like a skull and crossbones—reminded me of a Jolly Roger from a pirate ship.

George put me to work moving bags of soil, fertilizer, and grass seed from the warehouse to the garden center. When customers needed help, I loaded their vehicles. By the end of my shift, the idea of riding my bike all the way home was torture.

"You did all right today," George said as I clocked out.

"Thanks."

"Tuesday after school?"

"Yessir."

"Can you be here by four?"

"Yessir."

"Hey, kid, you can lay off the *sir* bit. I'm not all that much older than you."

"Okay."

"See you Tuesday."

I pedaled home, exhausted but satisfied. I showered, ate dinner, and was asleep before seven o'clock on a Saturday night. Every cell in my body ached.

SENTENCE STRUCTURE

Ryan stopped me at school. "Will accepted a plea agreement on reduced charges. Now he's in prison."

"Saw it in the paper," I said. "He needs to be locked up."

"I wonder how long it'll be till he gets paroled."

"I hope he screws up and never gets paroled."

"He'll screw up," said Ryan. "He's Will."

"Did you go to his hearing?"

"No. But my neighbor works in the state's attorney's office and he told my father."

"I'm glad we didn't end up having to testify," I said.

Ryan hesitated. "I don't know, Connor . . . I might have enjoyed watching him squirm for a change."

"Yeah, maybe."

Daniel's mother came to see me. I was hesitant to meet her eyes, honey brown just like Daniel's. She was so pale and quiet that she was barely even a shadow.

Mom abandoned me with her. I did not know what to say. The music in my head played soft melancholy songs but I could still hear the subtle vibrato in her voice when she spoke.

Daniel's mother talked about how she missed her son, and how she knew I did too. Her voice was tears and grave-yards. She reminisced about Daniel and his journey from infancy to childhood to the brink of manhood. She wept and took my hand. I cried too. Or did I? My memory is fragmented.

Upon leaving, Daniel's mother urged me to visit her sometime, claiming that seeing me made her son seem nearer. I didn't know if I could actually stop by her house. She gave me a brown paper grocery bag filled with Daniel's things. I took the bag to my room, where I slipped it into my dresser drawer without looking inside.

There was only one other kid in my age range working at Manulet's. He worked in the tool section. One day when I took a pallet of topsoil to the lawn-and-garden pavilion, I found him perched on top of the stack I'd already stocked. "Am I in your way?" he asked, sipping on a Red Bull. "I hope not, 'cause I'm not moving. I'm on break and it's hotter inside than it is out here. The cooling system's screwed up."

"No problem," I answered as I began to unload the pallet, stacking this load next to the one he sat on.

"So you're the new kid? What's this, your second week here?"

"Third."

"I've been here since last summer. Started out in the paint department. Totally sucked. Don't go there if you're asked. People are very particular when it comes to color."

"I'm okay with what I'm doing now," I said as I yanked a bag from the pile. It burst open and topsoil streamed everywhere. " 'Cept when that happens."

"I'll get the broom," he said, sliding off his earthen throne. He returned a couple of minutes later. "Here."

As I swept up the soil, he introduced himself. "I'm Jesse."

"I'm Connor."

"So how'd you get this job?"

I wondered if he, too, had been sent by Mr. Driver. "Came in and talked to Elwood," I answered evasively. "He hired me on the spot."

"He's all right. As bosses go, anyhow. I like working for him."

Jesse had the kind of open smile that made you believe he liked everyone. I'd already observed him charming customers and overheard other employees speaking well of him.

I dumped the wasted topsoil into an empty cardboard carton and handed him the broom. "Thanks."

"No prob." He glanced at his watch. "See you. Break's over." He tossed the Red Bull can into the box of topsoil.

PALS

There we were, Trent and I, in our little swimsuits with huge towels draped over our narrow shoulders. My trunks were printed with bright blue and green sharks, and Trent's had Buzz Lightyear and Woody, from Toy Story. "Come on, boys and girls. Time for the minnows," said the girl in the red swimsuit as she led us to the side of the pool.

"I already know how to swim," Trent announced.

"Me too," I said, and then a couple of other kids chimed in.

"Well, then I'll teach you how to swim better. Who can blow bubbles?"

"I can," answered Trent, always eager to be the leader. So she had him demonstrate what must be the fundamental skill required for swimming because it was the first thing we did.

While I sat on the edge with my feet dangling in the water, I looked across to the deep end. James was dancing down the high dive without a trace of trepidation. Suddenly he was airborne, twisting and flying, looking totally uncoordinated, and then he slapped the water with a splash. When he surfaced, he laughed and called out to Mom what great fun it was. James amazed me. It seemed as though nothing frightened him, ever.

After Trent's bubble demo, everyone had to take a turn. The kid next to me started crying and clinging to the side of the pool. The instructor tried to pry him away, and he began to kick (another necessary skill, but it hadn't yet been introduced). Trent was sitting on my other side. "He's scared," he said, stating the obvious.

"Yep."

"It's no different from being in the bathtub," Trent told the kid. The kid looked at Trent as if he knew darned well this was way different from being in the bathtub.

" 'Cept you're not naked," I added. The kid checked to make sure he was still wearing his swimsuit.

After the lesson, Trent and I joined Mom and James at a picnic table. "Piece of cake," said Trent.

"Easy cheesy," I added.

Mom laughed and James threw his flip-flops at us.

HARDWARE MUSIC

After the first couple of weeks at Manulet's, the job didn't wear me out or leave my muscles sore. The people were friendly and the atmosphere laid-back.

Elwood started calling me Strings when I showed up for work one afternoon following my lesson with Mr. Danescu. "That a machine gun?" he asked with a wink when he saw the violin case in my hand.

I grinned. "No. Just my violin."

"So the rumors were false. You're not a Mafia hit man?"

I laughed. "No. Just a music student."

Elwood never mentioned the fact that I was on probation. I wondered if Mr. Driver had given him my full story, or if my attitude on the job meant more to him than my past.

I mainly worked alone—keeping the outdoor covered pavilion stocked with everything from cement birdbaths to lawn furniture and organic mushroom compost. On really busy days, much of my time was occupied loading customers' vehicles. Occasionally I'd get tipped a couple of bucks. One lady who must have been at least as old as my mother creeped me out by handing me a slip of paper with *Alice* and a phone number written on it. I threw it away, but not before showing it to James, who called me the teenage gigolo for the next few weeks.

It surprised me how much I liked working at Manulet's. When I'd taken the job, I'd mainly done it to please Mr. Driver and pay off my debt to my father. I hadn't expected to find such satisfaction in it.

It was new for me to have a place in my life where I was simply Connor—not someone's brother, son, student, or friend. I came to Manulet's with no history. No one compared me to Trent or James, measuring which of the brothers was the better athlete, student, or whatever. No one cared how my parents made their livings. I wasn't acceptable or unacceptable because of the kids I associated with. The people there took me as I was, independent of my family, friends, or past.

Stocking inventory, a fairly brainless activity, allowed me to slide deep into my thoughts. Sometimes I'd run through a musical composition, exploring the subtleties the composer had used to set the mood of the piece. It was while unloading several shipments of fruit trees that I internalized my recital piece, a Spanish dance. Its melody was already in my head. I absorbed its spirit, a much more elusive thing, as it played at the edges of my consciousness while I worked.

In the warehouse, I started composing my own music—short phrases that teased my fingers and mind. I kept a notebook in my locker, and sometimes rushed over to scribble down the notes before unloading that next pallet of terracotta planters or Weed Eaters.

I'd be anxious to get home—to stroke out those new melodies on my violin. I'd refine them, combining, altering, and deleting. I'd add pizzicato or staccato or slurs. I had learned enough music theory to know the structural rules of music, but I didn't have the perspective to decide whether or not what I'd written had potential. One day, without telling him it was mine, I played Stewart a short piece I'd written.

"That's nice. Bittersweet," he said. "What is it?"

"Doesn't have a name."

"Who wrote it?"

I smiled and blushed. "I did."

"No kidding?"

I nodded. "Took me a while. I'm still working out the bugs."

"It's really good, Connor. Play it for Mr. B."

"No. It's not ready for public consumption."

He laughed. "Well, it's definitely good."

"Thanks."

"Maybe you'll be the next Mozart."

"Not much chance of that. Mozart started composing when he was like . . . five or something, so I'm already ten years too late. But I had fun writing it—sort of a high if that makes sense."

"It does. Play it again."

TORRENT

I sat on the rocks with Quicksilver. The wind was fierce—like blaringly loud heavy metal music. The ocean kissed me with its breath of salt. I gazed toward the horizon, searching the sea and sky for what was lost. I trembled with the cold. The dragon king wrapped his wings around me—reptilian blankets against the chill arctic wind. His heartbeats were eighth notes. His inhalations and exhalations were whole notes. He sang for me a haunting lullaby and rocked me gently.

Uncle Pete sat on the sofa. "You sound pretty good," he said, nodding toward the violin in my hand. "That your recital piece?"

"No. This is just one of those exercises Mr. Danescu assigns. It's nothing special."

"I need some help this weekend. I have to dismantle that show at Kirkwood's Gallery. Can I count on you?"

"Gotta work Saturday, but I've got Sunday off."

"Sunday's good. What about Trent? Think he'll help?"

"You better ask him. He's . . . well, I'd better not speak for him. He and I aren't getting along so great lately."

"You doing okay, Connor?"

His eyes made me self-conscious so I looked away. "Yeah."

"No you're not. You're my nephew—I can tell. But I guess if I was you, I'd be pretty slammed too."

I didn't say anything; just stroked out a simple melody on my instrument.

Once again, I woke up with my limbs shaking and my cold body bathed in droplets of sweat. It was that same dream—the one that repeatedly terrified me into sleeplessness. I sat up. It felt as if Will was in the room, filling it with his poison. And his eyes, always like ice and fire, overflowed with rage and scorn and something else I couldn't name—something pitiful—resignation maybe.

Shards of that dream lurked just out of my reach. Graphic flashes of Daniel and Will and the gun. Noisy and full of explosions and flaming red pain. I didn't know how to keep the dream from returning—how to disintegrate its power over me.

I wandered into the family room. James was sitting on the sofa flipping through the channels. "What's up?" he asked.

"Nothing. Couldn't sleep."

"Me either." He clicked the remote and the screen went blank. "Wanna go for a ride?"

"Sure."

It was a cold, drizzly night. The streets were slick and deserted. After cruising listlessly around town, we decided to check out the action beneath the interstate. Neither of us really had our heart in it, though, and when everyone else moved to the edge of the service road, where a Nissan was lined up against a classic Chevy Malibu, James and I stayed back. Rainwater oozing from the roadway above dripped down on us. "I've been on one long losing streak," James said. "I think the Camaro needs hospitalization."

"What's wrong with it?" I asked as the two drivers revved their engines at the starting line.

"I dunno. I think I need to rebuild the carburetor and adjust the timing."

There was a burst of engine noises and the smell of burnt rubber on asphalt. The two cars were rapidly gaining speed as they roared down the road. I glanced toward the finish line, then grabbed my brother's arm. "James. Cops," I whispered, my voice unsteady. I motioned toward the two cruisers that had pulled up at the other end of the service road. As I spoke, blue lights began to strobe, casting electric highlights and shadows on the tangle of wet freeways and cement supports.

James straightened and then said, "Take off. I'll pick you up on Addison Road. At the Circle K." We both knew what was at stake for me if this ended badly.

Sticking to the shadows, I walked in the opposite direction from the one where the police cruisers were gathered. As the distance between me and the cops increased, the flashing lights grew fainter and softer, leaving the flat planes of the concrete pylons washed in pale splashes of ethereal blue. Water droplets gathered in my hair. It was all I could do not to run, but I knew that would attract attention. The streets were very quiet, with only the sound of the rain and an occasional passing car.

I slinked to the side of the Circle K to wait for James, wondering if he'd been stopped. I'd expected him to arrive there before me. My arms were covered in goose bumps, either from the cool rain or from my jangling nerves. James pulled up just as I was about to panic, his windshield wipers lazily clearing the glass. "Get in," he called. I raced across the parking lot and jumped into his car. "What a stroke of luck that I parked behind that abandoned auto-body shop. I was able to get away undetected," he said as he slowly cruised home.

The squirrelly feeling in my guts hadn't yet disappeared. "That was a close one."

"I know, Connor. But it's all cool."

"What about those other guys?"

"I dunno. They know it's every man for himself. But don't worry, they'll be back. It's in their blood."

Trent and I were at the reservoir one evening last summer. We were skateboarding with some kids he hung out with. "Isn't that Daniel?" asked Trent, pointing across the water. I looked at the opposite embankment. Daniel and Will were talking to a couple of girls I didn't know.

Trent nudged me. "Want to go see what he's doing?"

I hesitated. Even from a distance, Daniel seemed like a stranger right then. His gestures were somehow false. He kept messing with his hair, squaring his shoulders, and frantically jiggling his right leg. Things not natural to Daniel. Then I shifted my gaze to observe Will. Daniel, I realized, was mimicking Will's movements.

"Let's go," Trent urged.

We started for the other side. "I hate how Daniel acts when he's with Will," I said.

Trent missed a kick flip and his board clattered onto the cement.

"Smooth," I said. Then I tried one and messed up.

"Even smoother." Trent laughed as I retrieved my board.

"Yo, Daniel," I called.

"Well, if it isn't Connor. With his babysitter," said Will derisively. "Oops, I mean baby sister."

"You're too hilarious," I said.

"The little girl speaks," jibed Will.

"What's your problem, Stanton?" Trent asked flatly.

"Hey, man, your mommy lets you stay out this late?" Daniel said with a laugh, slapping my back. The girls giggled.

I stepped away from him. "No. We're breaking curfew— living dangerously. Come on, Trent. Let's take off."

"I was just kidding," said Daniel. There was an apology in his eyes, but also maybe a sneer. Daniel said something else, but I didn't know what because Trent and I had taken off and the wheels of our skateboards scratched noisily at the rough pavement.

Two days later, Daniel appeared at my front door. "Whassup?"

"Whassup wit you?" I leaned against the doorjamb.

"Nothin'. Wanna go shoot some hoops?"

"I guess." I grabbed my shoes off the bedroom floor and sat on the front steps to put them on.

"You and Trent going to the reservoir tonight?"

"Dunno. Why?"

"I might be there."

"Well, if you're with Will Stanton, stay away from us."

"He went to his cousin's house for the weekend."

"Oh, I get it . . . your delinquent pal's out of town so you wanna hang with me."

"No. I'm sick of Will anyway."

"I've heard that line before," I muttered.

"Well, it's true."

"Then why do you act like him?" I asked.

"I don't."

"Right, Xerox." I stood up and grabbed the basketball from the bushes.

JOURNEY

I stood on her doorstep—my heart pounding madly—hoping she would not answer my knock. I wanted to abort this mission and not see her eyes, so like Daniel's. This place was very familiar to me, but foreign as well, now. It was greatly changed. Not the physical side of it—the flagstone steps, the border of red begonias, and the brass mailbox were all the same. It was the energy field that was different.

She opened the door and her face broke into a smile. "Connor, come in. I'm so pleased to see you." I followed her into the house and down the hallway to the kitchen, where she and Daniel had spent much of their time. In the doorway, she turned and hugged me. "It's so quiet here, Connor. I'm glad you came."

I sat at the table. I noticed Daniel's childhood artwork framed and hanging on the walls. Hopeful—like promises. But terribly sad, too. Broken promises.

She went to the refrigerator and took out the orange juice, pouring a glass and setting it in front of me. When she sat down, her hands hovered on the tabletop, lost and lacking in confidence.

"I came to see you to . . ." I didn't know how to finish what I was saying.

"I'm glad, Connor. To you, it might seem like nothing, but it means everything to me." She smiled weakly. "Things are so vague without Daniel. So many dreams and wishes have to be rearranged." I must have looked puzzled, because she explained herself. "You'll understand one day . . . graduations, girlfriends, college, jobs, marriage, grandchildren . . . I saved his things ever since he was a baby . . . clothes and toys and books, drawings and poems and stories . . . for the grandchildren I'll never have." She turned her face away from me.

I spoke softly. "I'm sorry. I miss him. It's lonely without him."

With her index finger she slowly traced the flower pattern woven into the fabric of the tablecloth. Then she sighed wistfully and said, "I know it's hard, Connor, but you're young. You have the world at your feet. It would delight me to know you were happy."

I hesitated and looked out the window to avoid her eyes.

I had to say it. It had been eating away at me for months—ever since that night. "But . . . don't you hate me? I was there. I should . . . should have done something. I knew it was dangerous . . . insane. But I did nothing."

"That's right, Connor. You did nothing. You didn't pull the trigger. And I hate to admit it . . . but Daniel . . . he made choices that night. He could have left. But he stayed. I know you wish you could turn back the clock . . . I wish that too. How desperately I wish that. I knew Will was bad news, but still . . . still . . . I let Daniel go with him. It eats at me in my sleepless hours. I should have kept him home that night."

"You couldn't have known what would happen," I protested.

"No. But my instincts told me Will was trouble." Her voice quavered. "Connor, I believe everyone involved has enormous regrets. Hopefully Will most of all."

"Doubtful," I mumbled.

"You can't know what's in his heart. So many lives changed forever in that one moment."

"I feel so guilty."

"You shouldn't. And I could never hate you, Connor. You made my son smile and laugh and shine. You were his best friend. You let him be someone he needed to be. Thank you for that."

After Daniel's shooting, my father raved at me, repeating the same few questions over and over. "How could you do such a thing?" "What were you thinking?" "Why didn't you do anything to stop it?" "Why didn't you leave?" I tried to give him answers that would help him understand—help me understand—but the reality is that I have no answers to those questions.

Once he got past his rage, Dad dealt with me in an efficient manner, discussing the legal repercussions of my involvement. Along with his file folder stuffed with news articles and official documents regarding my case, he had a calendar on which he noted any phone calls or meetings concerning the incident.

He was worried about what other people thought—friends, neighbors, relatives. Worried that they defined all of us by that one event.

I understood his anger, disappointment, and helplessness. My father is a scientist. He deals with problems methodically. First, identify the problem. Second, use the available data to isolate the facts. Third, explore possible solutions. Fourth, choose the most reasonable or likely solution. Fifth, if you fail, go back to the first step. His trouble was this: He couldn't get past step one; couldn't clearly identify the problem. It eluded him. So he was frozen. Immobilized.

Finally, though, bit by bit, he started to forgive me. He became less cold and hard when he spoke to me, and occasionally questioned me about something other than legal stuff. He wandered in to listen when I practiced my music, or sat with me on the sofa when I was idling away my time watching TV or listening to CDs.

BREAK

Jesse often spent his breaks in the garden center. If I was working in only one area, he'd find a perch and stretch out to relax. If I was moving around the pavilion, he'd follow me, usually talking nonstop. I was seldom required to contribute much to our conversations, but I enjoyed it when he came around.

One day he flung himself into a lawn chair with a Jones Twisted Lime soda in one hand and a Hostess Twinkie in the other.

"Nice healthy lunch today, Jesse?" I asked.

He laughed. "Yep. I always try to eat right and get plenty of exercise."

"Sure."

"Man, I'm so sick of people. Some of 'em ask the dumbest questions. Had a guy today who wanted to know if he could use a chain saw on corrugated aluminum. I 'bout said, 'Only if you're suicidal.' "

"So did you sell him the chain saw?"

"Course. Our best one. But I told him it wasn't recommended for metal. And to read the instruction manual. Which he won't. I'm sure we'll be hearing about him on the news sometime this week. He'll probably try to brush his teeth with it."

"Let's hope not."

He popped the second half of the Twinkie into his mouth. "What time do you get off?" he asked.

"Six."

"Wanna go grab a burger after work?"

"Um . . . sure."

I met Jesse at the back door at quitting time. "I'll drive," he said.

"You'll have to." I pointed across the driveway to the fence where my bike was chained. "Unless you wanna ride on my handlebars."

"No thanks. Haven't done that since seventh grade."

We went to the Burger King down the road from Manulet's. I wasn't completely comfortable being there. Wasn't sure I was capable of the responsibilities of friendship.

Wasn't sure there was room in my head for such complications.

We slid into a plastic booth. "So you don't have your own set of wheels?" Jesse asked as he squeezed catsup on his fries.

"No. I'm only fifteen. Can't afford a car anyhow."

"Fifteen? I didn't know Elwood would hire anyone that young. I'm seventeen. And already out of school. Got my GED last summer. The world's an open road."

"You don't want to go to college?"

"Naw. I've got other fish to fry."

"Like selling power saws and screwdrivers?"

Jesse grinned. "Gotta start somewhere. Before you know it I'll be CEO of Lowe's or Home Depot."

"Remember us little guys when you get to the top," I said.

CHECKMATE

"I'll get it," yelled Kathleen as she ran through the house to the front door. James and I were playing chess in the family room. "He's in here," I heard Kathleen say. I looked up to see my probation officer standing in the doorway.

"Mr. Driver," I said, rising.

"Hello, Connor."

"Um . . . my parents aren't here. Dad's still at work and Mom's picking Trent up from baseball practice."

"This your brother?" He motioned toward James.

"Yessir. This is James. You met Kathleen last time." James stood up to shake Mr. Driver's hand.

"So you're a chess player?" Mr. Driver asked James.

"Sorta. I'm not that good," James said. "Connor nearly always beats me."

"He's reckless. Brings his queen out too early," I explained. "He always loses her."

Mr. Driver laughed. "I haven't played chess in years." He combed through his hair with his fingers. "Well, you boys behave. Keep 'em in line, Kathleen." He winked at her and turned around. James and I followed him to the front door.

"Bye, Mr. Driver," I said.

James shut the door as Mr. Driver walked away. "That's your probation officer?"

"Yeah."

"I'd pictured someone more threatening."

"He's all right," I said.

Seeing Mr. Driver at my house always seemed way out of context. When he showed up, I wasn't sure what to do or say. He never stayed long, but I wanted to have compartments for the different parts of my life. One compartment for family, one for violin, one for the whole Daniel thing, one for school, and so on. When the contents of one compartment spilled into another, it was like a collision of two planets—like something had jumped its orbit and traveled to a place where it didn't belong.

MINOR SCALES

"Guess you can't get it out of your head unless you write it down." I jumped at the sound of George's voice behind me.

"I . . . um . . . I was only writing myself a note," I explained, afraid I'd get in trouble for on-the-job composing.

"Yeah. I see you doing it all the time," he said.

I put my notebook in my locker and closed it. "Sorry. I won't do it anymore."

He laughed. "It's not a problem if it's just a quick measure here and there. If it gets to be a problem I'll let you know."

"You don't mind?"

"No. Wish I had stuff like that in my head. 'Bout all I have up there is women and whiskey and worrying over my mortgage payment."

"Guess I'll go back to work," I said, backing away from my locker.

"Good idea." George thumped my arm and walked off. "Oh, maestro, there's a truckload of bird feeders and outdoor thermometers coming in. Maybe they'll inspire a master-piece."

DEAD END

I parked the Camaro in the driveway and killed the engine.

James jumped out. "It's about time."

"What are you talking about?" I asked as I closed the door.

"This is the first time you've ever made a whole trip without stalling out at least once." He danced a little Irish jig. "I'm celebrating."

I grinned. "Guess I'm starting to get the hang of it."

"Took you long enough. You only burned through three clutches."

"Funny, James. And your clutch is fine."

He grabbed me and put me in a headlock. Before long we were both rolling in the grass as I tried to wriggle an escape. "Wimpy baby," he said.

I couldn't respond to his insults as his arm was crooked around my throat. I jabbed him in the ribs with my elbows. He started laughing. "Cut that out. It tickles."

I arched my back and flipped from his grasp. "Ha!" I jumped up and stepped away.

He rose and brushed the grass clippings from his hair and clothes. "Trent still being pissy with you?"

I sat on the steps. "Yeah."

"I don't know what his deal is. Bad stuff happens, and being angry doesn't fix anything . . . only makes it worse, really."

"I don't know what to do."

"Don't do anything. The harder you try, the more you play into his hands."

"You're probably right. But it's like Antarctica sharing a room with him."

I was on my way out—hoping to meet up with Jesse at Caraway's CD and Video Exchange, where he was trading in an old Nintendo game system for some music CDs. "Come talk to me, Connor," my mother said. I turned to meet her eyes, then followed her into the living room. She sat on the sofa.

"What's up, Mom?" I asked as I sat beside her.

"Nothing really. I just feel like we haven't talked lately. I know you're having a hard time. I want to know how you are doing—how you're handling things."

"I'm okay."

"I'm always here for you."

"I know, Mom. Thanks.

She took my hand—ran her index finger across my palm and fingers, absorbing my ridges, loops, and whorls. "You know, Connor, when you were born, and I first held you and looked into your eyes, all I wanted to do was protect you from the world. And when you were little, I mostly could. Now, though . . . you've outgrown my ability to shelter you, but I haven't outgrown my need. It hurts me to see you suffer and know I can't fix things."

"Mom, I'm all right. I don't need protecting."

"That's what you don't understand . . . you may not need

protecting, but I still need to protect." She hugged me and kissed my forehead, and my heart broke a little bit for her.

HAMMERED

"Connor, hand me that screwdriver."

I reached for the tool and gave it to Uncle Pete. Trent and I were helping him crate some paintings for shipment to a gallery in Denver. This was something we'd been doing for years. Usually it was fun, but the atmosphere that day was tense. Trent hadn't spoken one word to me, and I'd given up after being rebuffed several times. I held a board in place for Uncle Pete and watched him screw it to the frame we'd built.

"You boys are sure quiet today," he commented.

"Nothing to say," muttered Trent.

"You mad about being here? You're not getting too grown up to help me out, are you?"

Trent looked embarrassed. "No. Just tired."

Uncle Pete raised his eyebrow. "You don't look tired."

Trent grunted. "Okay, then, moody."

"You look moody. What's eating you?"

"Nothing in particular," Trent replied evasively.

"It's 'cause I'm here," I said. I knew I was ratting Trent out, but I didn't care. I was sick of being treated as if I was invisible.

Uncle Pete leaned toward Trent. "He's your brother," he said. "What's your problem?"

"He doesn't know what he's talking about," said Trent. "Thinks everything's about him." He didn't look at Uncle Pete when he spoke. Instead he took a handful of nails from a box and lined them up like railroad ties on the workbench in front of him.

Uncle Pete watched Trent for a moment. Then he turned to me and said, "Connor, cut that plywood to size while I drill out these two-by-fours." I laid a sheet of plywood across the sawhorses and measured it. Trent kicked the leg of the workbench hard enough to rattle the nails and cause some of them to rain to the floor. "Trent, secure that board while Connor rips it down," directed Uncle Pete.

Trent rolled his eyes before reluctantly rising.

"I don't need help," I said, reaching for the circular saw.

"Oh, you need serious help, believe me," snapped Trent, "and I don't mean with that plywood."

Uncle Pete put down the drill and stood with his arms crossed in front of him. He looked hard at me, then at Trent. "The two of you should take it outside," he said. "Maybe beat the tar out of each other and call it a day."

I didn't want to meet Uncle Pete's eyes. Instead I stepped toward Trent. "Yeah. Wanna step outside?"

Trent glared at me. "You're not worth the trouble."

Before I knew what was happening, Trent was on the floor and Uncle Pete was pulling me off him. "Not in here," he said. "This is my studio, not Madison Square Garden. Take it outside."

Trent stood up and straightened his clothes. "You go to hell," he snarled. I wasn't sure if he was talking to me or Uncle Pete. He stomped to the other side of the studio and threw himself into an upholstered armchair.

"We're done for today," said Uncle Pete. "Go get in the van."

SONG WITHOUT WORDS

I was composing a new piece. My most daring yet. I called it "Ladder of Glass." Inspired by the vision that slipped uninvited into my nightmares and daydreams, where an icy landscape of blues, from palest tints to resplendent ultramarines to tones nearly black, rolled out across a barren plain. The stark horizon was broken only by a ladder reaching for the sky. A glass ladder.

The first movement was written in G major. I visualized

myself crossing the frozen plain to approach this ladder, knowing I was accepting a challenge essential to my survival. As I touched the first rung, the last note, played pizzicato, sounded.

The second movement was written in E minor, which I always found wistful. I stroked the strings of the violin, feeling the slap of the wind on my flesh. As I scaled the ladder, the glass flexed beneath my feet, threatening to shatter. My fingers slipped on the rungs. Everything depended on reaching the top, but I was drawn to the safety of the icy ground below.

The third movement came with less ease. I tried a number of variations. First I played in joyous waves as the ladder fell away and I took wing. Next I wrote in a crescendo of shattering glass that echoed in the blue universe. Last, I wrote in defeat as I descended the ladder.

None of these movements felt complete or true. I was stuck. Where did this vision lead? Was I supposed to retreat to the safe ground below, reach the top, or allow the glass to break beneath me?

Kathleen's ninth birthday. Everyone was on their best behavior. Trent wouldn't look at me, but he restrained himself from the usual sarcastic remarks he slung in my direction. Dad reminded me of a department store Santa Claus—hearty and cheerful, but not altogether comfortable in his disguise. Mom was dressed up pretty and smiling, but her smile was brittle. James adopted the role of social director—making sure everyone had something to drink or eat. Me, I tried to stay off the radar.

And Kathleen? She was no fool. She knew it was all a show—all stage props and scripted lines and lighting. But she, too, played her role. The smiling birthday girl—the guest of honor.

So we made it through Mom's carefully prepared dinner, and candles and ice cream and cake, but it all broke down when Kathleen unwrapped her gifts. She slipped up and said, "Remember last year, Daniel gave me eight silver dollars. I still have them. I wonder if he'd have given me nine this year, and then ten, and then eleven—"

That's when Trent could hold back no longer, and said, "There aren't any silver dollars where Daniel is now."

Kathleen started to cry and muttered she was sorry, and Mom tried explaining that it was really good to talk about

Daniel even though he was *gone*. Dad glared at Trent for ruining things, while James and I cleared away the dishes and cleaned the kitchen in silence.

Later, when she'd gone to bed, I went into Kathleen's room and sat beside her, stroking her hair in the darkness.

"Kathleen, thank you."

"For what?"

"You're the only one who talks about Daniel. You remember the good things, the special things."

"I don't want to forget him, Connor. He was my friend too."

"It's good to remember him. If everyone forgets him, then it's all totally meaningless."

"Maybe no one forgets. Maybe they just pretend."

"You're probably right. I wonder why that is?"

"Maybe they're afraid, Connor . . . 'cause it hurts."

"Do you think it ever stops hurting?"

"I hope so."

Trent dropped his backpack on the floor. "I always thought you were smart. How'd you end up on Will's roof that night? How'd you let that happen?" he asked.

I didn't look away from the book I was reading. "I didn't *let* it happen, Trent. I couldn't stop it."

"You didn't try."

"You weren't there."

"Straight. I wouldn't have been. I'd have left."

"I wish I had. I couldn't."

"You *could've*. You *didn't*."

I spoke softly, maybe more to myself than to him. "You don't get it."

"That's the truth. I sure as hell don't get watching someone blow my best friend's head off."

His words were slaps. I tossed the book aside and sat up. "You think I enjoyed it? That I wanted it to happen? Trent, I just didn't know how to make it stop."

"Ever hear the word *no*?"

"It wasn't like that. Daniel and Ryan, they laughed at me. They *wanted* to do it." I tried to meet his eyes but he avoided me.

"Right. Like Daniel wanted to die."

"No. Of course not. I don't think he believed he could

die. I don't think any of them thought it was real. It was a game to them."

"And you played."

"You weren't there. You don't get it."

Trent didn't say anything. He picked up his CD player and stuck the headphones in his ears. I reopened my book but couldn't concentrate on the words. I held it before my face like a shield.

"I saw you at school with Stewart Anthony. You running with him these days?" Trent asked after a few minutes. I glanced at him. He'd removed the headphones and was facing me.

"Some. We play guitar in orchestra class."

"You're playing guitar now? Why didn't you tell me?"

"Didn't seem important."

"Why not?"

His question astonished me. "Trent, it's not like . . ." I shrugged. "I didn't think it mattered. You barely even look at me. Why would I expect you to care about my music or anything else?"

He began to juggle a soccer ball with his feet and knees. "You're still my brother."

"DNA," I replied flatly.

"What?"

"That's just DNA. Biology. We used to run together. Talk. Do stuff."

He kicked the ball across the room. It bounced against my chest of drawers. "I guess I was mad at you."

"Whatever," I replied.

"So where'd you and James go after school today?"

"He took me to Mr. Driver's office."

"Where'd you go after that?"

"Cruising around. Stopped at Zack's place for a while and then went to Pep Boys for an air filter."

"What a bore."

"Wasn't so bad," I said.

"You two never include me. You're always off on your private little adventures."

I looked at Trent. "You can't be serious."

"Yeah, I am. I'm always left out."

"It's your choice, Trent."

INVITATION

I went with Quicksilver to his lair. His treasures were vast. Glittering gemstones cast their reflections against the shiny surfaces of golden goblets, chalices, and platters. Strings of pearls and crystals spilled from heavy chests.

Quicksilver led me to his carved marble throne and sang my secret name. On a low table was a silver box studded with amber and sapphires. Engraved on the lid was

Connor Kaeden. Quicksilver opened the box. I turned away. I did not want to look inside. I was afraid of what it might contain.

Again Quicksilver spoke my secret name. He held the box out to me. His eyes glittered with magic, and his breath was cinnamon and vanilla. He sang a mystery.

I looked into the box. It was empty.

GPA

"Your report card came in the mail today," my mother said, handing me a slip of yellow paper.

I groaned, then glanced over what I already knew.

"Connor, you failed English and geometry this quarter. English, of all things. I'm an English teacher. And you're barely passing your other classes."

"I got an A in orchestra."

She looked at me as though I was being flippant. "Yes, you did. I don't think one A will get you into college."

I stood there, saying nothing.

"Well?" She crossed her arms.

"Well what?"

"What has become of your ambitions? You used to strive

to succeed. You used to talk about music schools and scholarships."

"I dunno. Haven't thought too much about that stuff lately. Seems meaningless."

"That's defeatist talk. You know your future isn't meaningless. And you know you have the ability to excel. You can't afford another bad semester."

"It won't change things . . . not the real things."

"It won't change what has happened. But there are other real things. Part of who you are is the choices you make. If you make the choice to fail, it will define you. Is that who you want to be?"

"I'll try to do better . . . turn in my work and stuff," I said, telling her what she wanted to hear.

"You *must* do better. Much better. Connor, I know Daniel's death has been horrible for you. It was a terrible tragedy. But it's time for you to reconnect. The world isn't going to stop to wait for you."

"Can I go now?" I asked. I didn't want to have this conversation. I'd heard it all before.

"Yes, go," she answered with an exasperated sigh, as if she had a lot more to say but knew I'd just tune her out. "But I'm serious about your schoolwork."

SIXTEEN

Jesse had some friends whose garage band was playing at an outdoor concert at the downtown arts complex one Friday night. My parents were reluctant to let me go.

"Why not just build a cage and throw him a handful of seeds and mushy fruit now and then?" said James from across the room.

"That's enough, James," said my mother, but I could see he had made his point. My parents compromised, insisting they wanted to meet Jesse before consenting. He dropped by the house one night after work, charming them with his easygoing manners and crooked smile.

"Jeez, your parents are sure protective. You'd think I was your prom date," he teased. I didn't explain the reasons they were so cautious. Didn't want him to know about that part of my life.

At Stingray's after the concert, we ordered cheeseburgers at the counter and sat in a booth near the window to wait for our food. "How about that bass player with the frizzy hair and the tiki tattoos?" Jesse asked.

"He practically brutalized his instrument," I said.

"I'd like to play one of those . . . wait a sec, there's Elisa. She used to live across the street from me." He got up. "Back in a flash."

I sat gazing out the window, running through a difficult movement from my recital piece in my head. I did that when I was having trouble with a piece. Working through it without my instrument often smoothed the rough edges.

"Connor?" I turned to see Ryan standing at the table. "Mind if I sit here a sec?"

I shrugged. "No problem."

He slid into the seat across from me. "Tomorrow's Daniel's birthday," he said. "He'd be sixteen. It's weird, but I keep wondering if his dad would have really bought him a car. Remember he promised him one?"

"Yeah." I dragged my index finger across the Formica tabletop. "I keep thinking about his mother. Must be awful for her."

"Yeah. Must be."

"Should we do something?"

"What do you mean?"

"I don't know. Call her or go see her or something?"

"Jeez, Connor, I couldn't do that. I wouldn't know what to say."

"Me either."

Jesse appeared with our burgers. Ryan scooted out of the booth. "See ya."

The next day, Saturday, I worked all day. When I got off at four, I went home and took a shower. "I'm going out for a while," I told Kathleen. "Tell Mom I'll be home by eight." I bought some sunflowers from a vendor at the curb market. I walked to Daniel's house, standing idly on the porch for several minutes before I had the nerve to knock. Everything was very still.

When Daniel's mother opened the door, I could see that she'd been crying. Her face was swollen and her eyes bloodshot. The house was dark inside; the only light shone from a dim lamp burning in the living room. The place echoed with emptiness. "I've . . . um . . . been thinking about you today," I said uncertainly.

She didn't answer. Just stood there in the doorway.

"Since it's Daniel's birthday and all."

She averted her face and swept her hand across her eyes.

"I brought flowers." I held them out. She took them listlessly and then dropped her arm so that the blossoms brushed the threshold. "Well, bye, then," I said, not knowing what else to do. I hesitated a moment before walking away.

When I was almost to the street, she called, "Connor."

I turned around.

She forced a smile to her lips. "Thank you. You're a sweet kid."

"Um . . . you're welcome," I said.

She closed the door.

I went to the reservoir and sat on the embankment. People were engaged in their usual activities, but I felt detached from them. I thought about how, for Daniel and me, sixteen had seemed like a magic number—something to achieve. Driver's licenses and staying out later and girls, although how turning sixteen meant we'd suddenly get the girls I wasn't sure. It would be another two months before I turned sixteen. I wondered where I'd be—who I'd be—when that day came. I wondered at the frightening reality of never turning sixteen. "Happy birthday, Daniel," I whispered. "I miss you."

CURRENT

I stood in the doorway. James sat on the sofa tying his shoes. I glanced at the clock—1:07. The room was dark—lit only by the pale moonlight slipping through the slats in the blinds.

"James, what're you doing?"

"Going for a ride."

"You going racing?"

"Naw. Just driving . . . wanna come?"

"Yeah." I went to my room and grabbed my jeans.

"What's goin' on?" Trent asked, sitting up in his bed.

I looked at Trent and groaned. "Go back to sleep."

"What are you doin'?"

"Just going for a ride. Be quiet, would ya? Go back to sleep."

Trent followed me into the living room, where James was waiting with the keys in his hand. "Can I come?"

James hesitated and looked down the hallway. "Yeah, I guess, but be quiet."

We had not gone out together, just the three of us, since before that night on Will's roof. We climbed into the car and James backed out of the driveway.

"So, where're we headed?" asked Trent.

"Anywhere. Everywhere. Nowhere. We're just riding." James slipped a Porno for Pyros CD into the player. He turned it up loud and "Tahitian Moon" spilled from the vehicle. The sky was bright with stars.

We streaked through the night. James took the curves with ease and raced down the straightaways like electricity. I felt that surging sense of freedom that always washed through me on our adventures. We ended up on the river road. James pulled into a vacant parking lot, killing the engine.

We walked across the pavement to the river. The sandbank across the water was a bright white ribbon in the darkness.

James stood on a boulder just above the waterline. I stood beside him, with Trent on my opposite side. "You know, what happened to Daniel could have happened to almost anyone," James said slowly, tossing broken twigs into the current. "I've sure done some risky, stupid things. We all play with fire, one way or another, if we're really alive."

I wasn't sure if James was addressing me or Trent or himself. I watched the river roll toward the sea.

"Nice night, eh?" James added when neither Trent nor I commented.

When we got home, the moon was rising. I slipped to my island in its ocean of glass, thinking about Daniel, and playing with fire, one way or another, and being alive.

And my brothers. The two people who knew more about me than anyone else. My relationships with them had changed drastically since that night on Will's roof. Trent was finally beginning to forgive me—to allow me to have messed up, but understanding we could be friends in spite of it. I wondered if we'd ever again get back to the place we were before Daniel's death.

And now, James and I were closer than we'd ever been. I think he looked at me differently after that night—saw my flaws but related to them. Found someone in me he'd not seen before. Someone he recognized.

Jesse picked the blooms off the tray of marigolds in front of him and rained bright yellow and orange petals onto the concrete floor. "Last night was wild," he said.

"Don't tear up the merchandise. People like to know what the flowers look like," I replied.

He plucked another blossom and shredded it. "Oops." He laughed. "Another one bites the dust."

"Jesse, cut it out. Go trash your own area, not mine."

"Don't have an aneurysm. I'm just making sure you don't run out of things to do today." He pushed a row of potted bushes together to clear some space and sat down. "You've gotta stay busy on the job."

I laughed. "Thanks for your concern, but I've got plenty to do already."

"Guess what I did last night, Connor?"

"What?" I was picking up the petals littering the floor.

"Felt like Robin Hood."

"Robin Hood? As in Little John and the Sheriff of Nottingham?"

"Yeah. Just like that."

"What'd you do?"

"Me and my pal, Rocky, and his brother Derek drove

Rocky's truck around this ritzy neighborhood stealing stuff off people's porches."

"What kind of stuff?"

"Whatever. Chairs, statues, plants, decorations. But here's the thing. We replaced what we took with something from another house. Kinda like Robin Hood. 'Cept we stole from the rich to give to the rich. I wish I was a fly on the wall this morning. 'Cause when those people walk out today, their stuff'll be gone but strange stuff'll be in its place. At this one house, we took two wrought iron chairs but left these big cement geese. Then we put the chairs on the porch across the street. We took a huge potted fig tree from that house, and left it at the place around the corner."

"What's the point?" I asked.

"It was a joke. We were just bored."

"Wasn't it a lot of work, hauling that stuff back and forth?"

"Like I said, we were bored. And kinda trashed." He was chuckling to himself. "Can't you just imagine the neighbors accusing each other?"

"I guess."

"You shoulda been there, Connor. We laughed our heads off. We even snuck into someone's backyard. They had a pool with more junk crowded around it than we've got here in the entire lawn furniture section. Rocky got the idea to dump all the stuff into the pool. We were clearing the deck, as they say on board ship, but then we must've set off the alarm, 'cause all the outside floodlights came on and a shrill whistle sounded. Left a chaise lounge sitting on the diving board when we made our getaway."

"Did you get caught?"

"No. We hightailed it outta there. Derek's flip-flops fell off when he jumped the fence. Think they can use flip-flops as evidence?"

I shrugged. "How would I know?"

"Wish you'd've been there. It was hilarious. We laughed all the way home." He tore a rosebud from a bush and tossed a handful of pink petals into the air. They floated to the ground. I almost told him why I wouldn't, couldn't have been there. Almost told him about Daniel, Will, and the gun. But something stopped me. He checked his watch. "Back to work," he said. "See ya."

"Hey, Jesse?"

"Yeah?"

"On my break, I'm heading to the tool department. Think I'll rehang all the saw blades on the wrong racks just to make things interesting inside. Rearrange the fan belts, too. And maybe *accidentally* litter the floor with bolts and washers or something. Just to give you something to do."

Mom took me shopping for a blazer to wear to my violin recital. I had worn basically the same thing every year since I was six—khaki pants, white dress shirt, tie, and navy blue jacket. "You should invite Daniel's mother to your performance," she suggested.

I felt cold. "No, Mom. I couldn't do that."

"Why not?"

"It'd be too weird."

"Weird? How?"

"She's Daniel's mother, and he's dead, and I'm still here."

"She's lonely, Connor. She'd appreciate you sharing this with her."

"But Mom—"

"Connor, you were Daniel's closest friend. It would mean something to her."

"I've been to see her . . . isn't that enough?"

"Connor!"

"It's so hard, Mom. She's so . . . so . . . far away."

"The same could be said about you."

"Are you gonna make me ask her?"

"No. I'll let you make that decision."

James kneed the side of my mattress.

"What?" I asked, turning to look at him. I hadn't been asleep, but I wasn't completely awake, either. I'd been drifting somewhere between the two.

"Wanna go for a ride?"

I yawned. "Yeah, sure."

"Come on."

I pulled on some jeans and grabbed a T-shirt. "Let's go."

The night was moonless and the stars bright. "Shhh," said James when I slammed the car door.

I knew we were going racing by the direction in which James turned when he reached the light at the corner of Sinclair and Seventeenth. I felt that combination of fear and thrill I always felt those nights.

"Hey, James, how 'bout letting me drive tonight?"

"You?"

"Come on. Please."

He laughed. "You drive like an old granny."

"No, I don't. Or I won't. Not if I'm racing. I'll put the pedal to the metal. And it's a straight shot, so how wrong can I go?"

"Plenty wrong."

"Just this once. I'll never ask again. Please."

"Lemme think about it."

We parked next to a little import outfitted with neon under-car lights. James hopped out and was immediately embroiled in conversation with a number of people all at once. I leaned against the Camaro and watched. "Connor," called James, throwing me his keys. "You're up." Everyone turned to look my way. The keys smacked my palm in a jangle of eighth notes.

"What?" I asked.

"You heard me. You're gonna run against Doug."

"Yeah? Awesome." All their eyes were on me. Suddenly I found myself reconsidering. I hadn't really expected James to agree. The keys felt cold and hard in my hand.

"I'll ride shotgun," James said, sliding into the passenger seat.

I put the key in the ignition.

"Back it up and go to the line," James directed. "Next to the Honda. Doug's waiting."

My chest felt tight, my hands cold. I started the car and shifted into reverse. As I approached the starting line, I adjusted the mirrors.

"An optimist, eh? You think he'll be behind you!" teased James.

I shrugged.

James started giving me instructions but I barely listened. Not that I felt I didn't need his help. My blood was just pulsing so rapidly I couldn't focus on any one thing.

"Take a deep breath and clear your head," he said as I

pulled up next to Doug, who was anxiously revving his engine. "Think about nothing but your foot on the pedal and the road unfolding ahead of you. And haul ass."

People gathered at the starting line. A curvy girl with short black hair held a bright scrap of silk. She waved it with the flourish of a matador. Doug was off the line in an instant, but I froze.

"Punch it, Connor," yelled James.

I jammed the gas pedal and let out the clutch, afraid I'd stall. Instead the Camaro lurched forward and the distance between Doug and me narrowed.

"Shift," said James. "Now."

The car jumped erratically beneath my inexpert touch. I remembered the smooth rides with James and felt foolish. Doug was several car lengths ahead of me.

"Shift."

My heart thudded and my brow felt cold as beads of sweat formed there. My attention was momentarily distracted by something—I don't even know what. I jerked the wheel and we lost traction. The car slid across the pavement wildly. The pylons of the overpass flashed by us. James cursed. I jammed the brake, which caused us to spin in circles as the engine died and we spiraled to a halt.

"What the hell?" asked James, unbuckling his seat belt.

"Sorry," I said, shaken.

To my surprise, James began to laugh. "I didn't think you'd last that long."

"What?"

"Didn't think you'd make it thirty feet."

"Thanks a lot."

"Pretty scary, huh?"

My hands were shaking. "That's an understatement. Here, you drive."

"You play, you pay, Connor. You've still gotta cross the finish line."

"But Doug already won."

"You still have to finish the race. Start the engine."

"I feel like a fool," I told James. All the others had to be laughing at my failure. The last thing I wanted to do was slink across the finish line. "I just wanna go home."

"Do it. Now," said James. "No one cares. We all spin out sometimes."

I fired up the engine and drove across the finish line like a dog with his tail between his legs. Then I climbed from the car to shake Doug's hand and acknowledge his victory. He slapped my shoulder in a friendly way. I was glad when James and I took off a few minutes later.

The porch light was on when we pulled up to the house. "Did you turn on the outside lights?" James asked.

"No. I thought you did."

"This doesn't look good for the home team," he muttered as he killed the engine.

We were halfway up the front walk when my father's

silhouette appeared on the porch. James whispered, "Oh, crap. We're cooked." He raised the volume a few notches. "Hey, Dad. Nice night, isn't it?"

My father didn't speak or move. By now James and I stood at the bottom of the steps and Dad towered above us with his arms crossed. His face was mostly in the shadows, so I couldn't read his expression.

"We went out for a ride," James announced lightly.

"It's three a.m.," my father said flatly. "Hours past curfew."

"We couldn't sleep. Remember how you used to take us for car rides to settle us down when we were little? We thought we'd give it a try."

I wanted to tell James to hush because I knew Dad wasn't buying it. More likely, he found it condescending. Insanely, James kept going. "It worked, too. I could sleep like a baby now. Good night."

When he spoke, my father's voice revealed no humor. "Nice try, James. Now get in the house, both of you. Meet me at the kitchen table."

James, ever irrepressible, took the steps in one graceful leap as if he was clearing a hurdle. I knew better. I waited until my father turned toward the house and sedately followed him to the kitchen. James was already sitting at the table stirring Nestle's Quik into a glass of milk. "Want some?" he asked no one in particular. When neither Dad nor I answered, he shrugged.

"All right, where have you two been all night?" Dad asked as he pulled out a chair.

"Like I said, out riding around," answered James as he capped the milk carton.

"In the dead of night?"

"Like I told you, we couldn't sleep, so—"

"Can it, James. I'm not stupid."

For the first time James's demeanor changed. "Sorry, Dad. But we really were out riding—just cruising around. No harm done."

"James, use your head. If you'd been stopped, Connor'd have gone straight to jail. And you're breaking curfew yourself. Don't you get it? This is real life, where the price for one small mistake is huge. Now, where were you two tonight, Connor?"

How like my father to turn the tables and suddenly address me. I certainly couldn't tell him we were drag racing beneath the interstate. I thought back to the night Trent had joined us. "We rode out to the river, Dad. Sat on the bank talking. Then we came home." I didn't dare look at James. I was afraid if I did I'd blow it.

"Do you want to end up in jail, Connor? 'Cause if you do, you're going about it the right way."

"Jeez, Dad, no. I just didn't think about it like that. I mean, I was with *James*."

"You think that makes any difference? If anything, it makes it worse. Being led astray by your own brother."

"It's not his fault," I protested. "I wanted to go with him."

My father shook his head. "I don't know which of you is the bigger fool."

James set his empty glass on the table with a dull thud. "Dad, he can't be good all the time. Shouldn't have to. He's a kid. He oughta be able to have a little fun once in a while."

My father's remote anger was replaced with emotional rage and it was riveted on James. "Fun? You call it fun when it means he could blow his future? End up in jail being some con's pretty boy? You're his brother. You should be keeping him out of trouble, not leading him to it."

I couldn't sit there while James got blasted. "Dad, it's not his fault. I wanted to go. Asked to go."

My father looked at us as if we were hopeless. "I don't know which of you is the bigger fool," he said again. He laid his hand, palm up and open, on the tabletop. "Give me your keys, James."

"Aw, Dad, no," protested James.

"The keys. Now."

My brother reluctantly reached into his jacket pocket and dropped his keys into Dad's hand.

"Now go to bed. Both of you," said Dad. He sounded tired—not sleepy but weary. As if he'd had enough.

James gave me a friendly shove as we walked down the hall. It was nothing really, except it let me know he didn't hold losing his car keys against me. "Kyle Petty you're not," he whispered.

My father cleared his throat. We turned to see him standing at the other end of the hallway. "By the way, boys, you're both grounded. Indefinitely."

"Aw, Dad," James started to argue, but the look in my father's eyes silenced him.

SIX-STRINGS

It was another Friday afternoon. Stewart and I sat in our usual spot jamming on those low-grade guitars. We'd been playing together long enough by that point that we improvised. One of us would play a melody that the other would weave through until a new melody emerged. And another and another. It was creative fun, and we sounded pretty good. "So your recital, when is it?" Stewart asked.

"Next weekend."

"You ready?"

"I guess. Ready as I'll ever be."

"You nervous?"

I plucked the E string. "Yeah, a little."

"Can I come? I'd like to hear you play."

I felt as if a boa constrictor was wrapping itself around my chest.

"Connor?"

I slid the guitar from my lap. "No."

"I can't?"

"Stewart, all my family's going to be there. Even my uncle and his crew. And if that's not bad enough, Daniel's mother is coming. Not to mention all the people I don't even know. I can't handle any more than that."

He played a few riffs of "Smoke on the Water."

"You understand?" I asked.

"Yeah. Wanna learn some nineties grunge?"

"Sure."

He ran through several measures of a song. "One of my favorites. 'Angry Chair.' Alice in Chains."

I picked up my guitar and repeated what he'd done.

WINGS

Quicksilver called my secret name from the other side of the ice. I slipped through to sit with him. He held something out to me—a fiddle unlike any I'd ever seen. This one was made of glass. The strings were shafts of sunlight. I took it and my hands instantly felt comfortable against its cold, slick surface.

Quicksilver handed me the bow. This, too, was made of glass, and its strings were moonbeams. I touched the bow to the instrument. The music issuing from the fiddle was at once sweet and sad and bitter and salty and joyous. I fell into the music and lost sight of where I was. Even who I was. The music covered me like a blanket. It embraced me like the ocean. It swallowed me.

Quicksilver summoned me back from the music and took the instrument from my hands. It became an exquisite golden bird with a long, slender neck, a bird that flew away and disappeared behind the moon.

BASS CLEF

Stewart and I had just left Russo's Music, where he'd bought new strings for his violin. I'd never hung out with Stewart outside school before. I'd avoided it, actually. But I felt bad about the recital, so I agreed to a trip to the music store.

Trent was approaching us on the sidewalk. "What's up?" he asked, stepping on one end of his skateboard to flip it up so that he could grab it.

"Not much," I answered. "Stewart just blew a quick forty-five dollars on musical hardware."

Stewart laughed and held up the small packet of strings.

"Stewart, this is Trent. Trent, Stewart."

They exchanged greetings and made small talk. Finally, Trent said, "Well, I'm off. See you around," and dropped his skateboard on the sidewalk.

"So that's your brother?" Stewart asked as Trent rode away.

"Yeah. One of 'em."

"He doesn't look much like you, but you act the same."

"What? How so?"

"He moves like you. Talks like you."

I watched Trent disappear around the corner. It was nothing like looking into the mirror, and I wondered what Stewart had seen that connected us to each other.

MUSIC THEORY

When I was in eighth grade, I was a music-video junkie. The classical music I'd been studying with Mr. Danescu since my "Row, Row, Row Your Boat" days seemed obsolete.

Mr. Danescu had obviously dealt with this attitude in

155

other students. "So you think those composers were boring old guys who sipped tea and wore velvet and lace?" he asked.

"Exactly. I wanna get an electric violin and rock out."

"I see. Like Jimmy Page, Jeff Beck, or Eddie Van Halen, except on violin and not guitar?"

"*You* know who *they* are?"

"Naturally. Even attended a great Zeppelin concert in July of seventy-three. Front-row seats. Buffalo, New York."

"Wow."

"You are aware, aren't you, that Eddie Van Halen's son is named Wolfgang as a tribute to Mozart?"

"You're kidding."

"And many of these modern performers have extensive classical training . . . take Randy Rhoads, for example."

"Who's that?"

Mr. Danescu gave me that you-must-be-totally-clueless look. "Formerly of Quiet Riot, and later the guitarist for Ozzy Osbourne. Died when a plane brushed their tour bus with its wing. Excellent classical guitarist."

"How do you know all this stuff?" I asked.

"I live in the world with my eyes wide open, Connor. And I think the whole history of music is captivating—not just one brief movement." He took my violin from my hands. "I don't want you to practice at all this week."

"Not practice?" By now I was beyond shock. Mr. Danescu required his students to put in many weekly hours at the violin and knew immediately if they didn't. "Are you firing me?" He'd been known to dismiss kids for not being serious enough.

"Certainly not. Not yet, anyway." He pulled a hard-bound volume from his bookcase. "This week, you'll spend your practice time reading."

"*Lives of the Composers,*" I read aloud from the spine. I gawked at him. "You want me to read this stuff?"

"I do. Not all of it. But at least read about some of them. They weren't the stuffed shirts you seem to think they were . . . but you can decide for yourself."

"I'll practice," I said dully.

"No, you won't. Or you'll both practice and read. Those are the terms."

"But—"

"That's all, Connor. Madison is here for her lesson."

I left with the book in my hand.

That night I flipped listlessly through the pages, glancing at the biographies of the various composers. One was a prodigy, another was deaf. It all seemed a bit dry.

Then I started reading about Niccolò Paganini. As his history unfolded, I realized he could easily have been a modern rocker. Famous for pallid skin and wild dark hair that fell down his back, Paganini in performance often brought his audiences to tears, or occasionally, even to a state of hallucination. One listener actually claimed to have seen the devil guiding the violinist's bow onstage during an exceptionally intense concert. Paganini was a reckless gambler who once pawned his instrument to pay his gaming debts. Unable to play anymore, he borrowed a valuable violin from a patron and then refused to return it after the performance.

Like Jimmy Page, who used a violin bow to tease new sounds from an electric guitar, Paganini broke many established rules in the music world. Aside from tuning his instrument untraditionally and playing entire pieces on only one or two strings, Paganini was responsible for one of the most drastic changes in the history of the violin—he lengthened the neck of the instrument to increase its musical range. He wrote such complex compositions and played so violently and sweetly that many people believed he had sold his soul to Satan in exchange for his rare talent. I smiled to myself, thinking about the modern rockers aiming for the image Paganini acquired quite by accident.

I read up on other composers. Each had his own achievements and quirks. His own complicated story to tell.

When I returned for my lesson the following week, I handed Mr. Danescu his book. He led me not to his studio, but to what he called his burrow. We sat in upholstered chairs on either side of the fireplace. He gazed into the empty grate. "A dull bunch, weren't they? Hardly worth wasting time on."

"Well, actually—"

"I'm sure those prissy old guys have nothing at all to do with modern music."

"Well, actually—"

"And many music historians compare Paganini's impact on his society to Beatlemania in the nineteen-sixties. Can you imagine that?"

I began to tell him all about Paganini, as if he didn't already know the things I'd only just discovered.

"Bunch of boring old geezers," he said quite seriously. "You'd probably be better off playing the fiddle at a barn dance."

Finally I laughed. "You've made your point," I said.

"Shall we?" He led me back to his studio, where I took my instrument from its case and pulled the Bach portfolio out of my stack of sheet music.

STOPLIGHT

My mother braked for a red light. Since Dad had the keys to the Camaro, Mom took me to Mr. Driver's. She wasn't nearly as much fun as James. She wanted to discuss serious stuff and always asked a billion questions. "I'm glad to see you making new friends," she said.

"Friends?" I asked.

"Jesse and Stewart."

"They're just people, Mom, not necessarily friends."

She sighed. "Jesse seems like a nice kid. He's very outgoing."

"He's okay."

"Connor, tell me about Stewart."

"Stewart? He's cool. He's in orchestra with me."

"I know that. But what's he like?"

"He's a violinist."

"Connor, I know that." The light changed and she took a left when the traffic cleared. "What else?"

I turned my face toward the window. "What do you want to know?"

"I want to be informed about the people my children run around with, that's all."

"You think Stewart's bad news? You haven't even met him."

"I didn't say he was. And if I haven't met him it's because you haven't brought him around."

"To our own private little fun house?" I scoffed.

"Connor, don't be disrespectful."

"What about respecting me, huh? What about that?"

She stopped at another light. "We respect you and you know it."

"Right. That's why you always think the worst. All the time. *Where are you going? What are you doing? With who?*

Jeez. I'm sick of it." I jumped out of the car and slammed the door.

I got home a couple of hours later. By then, my anger had abated and I was ashamed to have behaved so badly. My mother was grading compositions. "Mom?"

She turned to look at me, her marking pen poised in the air.

"I'm sorry. I overreacted."

"All I did was ask about Stewart."

"I know. I'm just tired and . . . I don't know . . . stressed out."

"You aren't the only one experiencing those things."

"I know."

"Don't mumble. And Connor, you don't resolve conflicts by jumping out of the car."

"It was stupid."

"We've always asked you and your brothers about your friends and your plans. You know that." She put the composition in one of the two piles on the table. "My interest is nothing new."

"I know. But somehow it feels different now."

"Things are different, Connor."

"I'm sorry."

"I didn't mean to hurt your feelings about Stewart. Trent says he's a nice kid."

"Trent said that?"

"Yes."

CRITIC

"Wait. Lemme get this straight. You're taking off work for a *violin* recital?" Jesse asked, flipping a Cheez-It into his mouth.

"Yeah."

"On a Saturday afternoon?"

"I didn't schedule it, Jesse."

"So what. Elwood's putting me out here for the day. Me! His tool expert."

"Expert? I think Keith's the expert," I said, naming Jesse's manager.

"Whatever. I don't know squat about mole crickets or crabgrass."

"You'll survive. It's just one afternoon."

He popped open an orange soda and chugged a few gulps. "You're gonna stand in front of all those people playing that old-school sissy music while I'm out here sweating?"

"It's not sissy music," I protested with a laugh.

"It's not Metallica." He tilted the Cheez-It bag to his mouth to suck up the last few crumbs.

"For your information, some of their stuff uses violin."

"Oh yeah. Guess you're right. I forgot."

"As do lots of other bands."

"Yeah, yeah, yeah." He crumpled the empty Cheez-It bag and stuffed it into his pocket.

"So have fun Saturday, Jesse. Don't prick your finger on a rose thorn."

"What is it they say to performers? Break a leg?" He set the orange soda can on the concrete and smashed it. "See ya around, Beethoven."

"That's Mr. Beethoven to you, punk."

CUBISM

I retreated to my island in its ocean of glass. I waited for Quicksilver to come. At twilight, I heard the song of his scales in the wind and saw him swirling above me in bright brushstrokes.

He streaked across the sky and came to sit beside me. In his talons he held a painting. It was a portrait of Daniel, painted fractured and distorted like one of Picasso's cubist canvases. The painting frightened me, but I could not look away from it. Nor did I dare reach for it.

Then Quicksilver spoke one word to me, and although I did not understand his language, I understood what word it was.

Forgiveness.

PERFORMING ARTS

I straightened my tie and tuned my violin. Mr. Danescu's other students were absorbed in their own preperformance rituals. I felt a sense of dread. I wasn't afraid of the music. I had traveled its measures and explored its melodies even in my dreams. I was never afraid of the music, even when I was very young. It was the eyes that frightened me. Always the eyes.

They were all in the auditorium: Mom with her nervous pride, Trent with his righteousness, Daniel's mother with her vacancy, along with Dad, James, Kathleen, and Uncle Pete with his wife and stepdaughters. And the strangers. So many strangers. So many eyes.

When my turn came, I walked out, trying not to see

those eyes and wishing they couldn't see me. I paused, put my violin to my throat, and raised my bow. In the deepest, most private caves of my heart, I thought about Daniel, and our friendship, and the tangled mess left in the wake of our choices. The pianist waited for my signal, and then, exhaling, I played the first measure. I could feel my hands shaking. I could hear the desperation spilling from my instrument. So I closed my eyes and summoned Quicksilver, who calmed my heart's vibrato with his mysterious songs.

And finally, I stroked the final note. I bowed. The audience applauded as I thanked the pianist. I flashed Kathleen a shaky smile before going backstage. Mr. Danescu, following his tradition, shook my hand. I carefully dusted the spent rosin from the gleaming surface of my violin.

Later, I sat outside on the back stoop of the auditorium with James. "You played well," he said.

"Thanks. But I didn't really nail it—not like I have so many times. My hands betrayed me—trembling like that."

"No one knew. You couldn't tell."

"I knew."

Forgiveness. The word Quicksilver spoke when he presented Daniel's portrait.

I looked it up in the thesaurus. Lots of words followed it. *Absolution, acquittal, amnesty, clemency, condonation, dispensation, exculpation, exoneration, extenuation, grace, immunity, impunity, indemnity, justification, lenience, lenity, mercy, overlooking, palliation, purgation, quarter, quittance, remission, remittal, reprieve, respite, vindication.*

I've heard most of those words before, either in courtrooms or churches, sometimes on vocabulary tests. None of them rang true to me. I know that Quicksilver meant forgiveness when he spoke to me, but not any of those other words.

WHEELS

James grinned and put me in a headlock. "Finally got my keys back," he said, jangling them in my face.

"Oh yeah? Bet you got a pretty good lecture to go along with 'em. I got one of those myself. More than one actually. All about what could've happened and learning to think about the consequences before I act."

"I've gotten that one a few times over the years," said James. "So, wanna go racing tonight?"

"What? No way. Dad'll have his radar honed. And, James, I'm not doing it anymore. I hate to admit it, but he's right. I could end up in deep trouble. I was really being stupid."

"I was only kidding. I'm not going either. Not for a while, anyway." He tossed the keys into the air and caught them. "Don't wanna lose these babies again."

GATOR

I walked into Mr. Driver's office. He wasn't there, but the bottom drawer of one of his file cabinets gaped open. I was astonished by what I saw.

The drawer wasn't full of yellowed, obsolete files. It wasn't full of blank documents waiting to classify another youthful offender. It wasn't full of office supplies, or lunch, or even toothpaste and shaving stuff and clean shirts he might need during the day.

Mr. Driver's bottom drawer was full of plastic alligators. Some looked realistic, but many of them were outrageous colors. One was fluorescent orange and at least three feet long, with its scaled tail hanging out of the drawer.

Another had *New Orleans* stamped on its belly. It played a trumpet and wore a top hat.

Yet another looked as if someone had spilled a rainbow on it. A neon rainbow.

"Hello, Connor." Mr. Driver stood in the doorway. I looked at him hovering there in his rumpled clothing. Then I turned back to the drawerful of reptiles. "Do you like my collection?" he asked.

I was speechless.

He crossed the room and grabbed a handful of gators. Plastic tails, snouts, and legs poked out everywhere. He tossed them on the desk. "I started collecting them when I was in college in Florida," he explained. "I have hundreds now."

I stared at him, puzzled. This pale, faded man with such gentle eyes collected plastic alligators?

"Most of my gators are at home," he said proudly. I tried to imagine what his home was like. Did he have a wife, children, a dog? Did he live in a house? Apartment? I felt like a first grader. When I was little, I thought the teacher lived at school.

"Do you collect anything?" he asked me.

I shook my head.

"Pick out an alligator. You can have one. You don't have to collect them or anything."

I sifted through the gators and chose one. It was about four inches long and scarlet, with large yellow eyes and pointed rubber teeth. I thought maybe it would act as a talisman; a charm to keep my demons at bay. I slipped it into my pocket.

JUNKYARDS

I stood in front of the music stand, struggling through a difficult new piece. Kathleen lay belly-down on the rug, playing solitaire. The telephone rang—a note even more discordant than the measure I'd just massacred. Kathleen walked on her knees across the floor and picked up the phone. I listened with half an ear while I made some markings on my sheet music. "They're not here. What's going on? . . . Connor's with me. . . . Okay, okay, hold on." She brought me the handset. "James wants to talk to you. He's being bossy."

I put down my instrument and reached for the phone. "What's up?"

"I got in a wreck," James said in a shaky voice.

169

"You okay?" I asked.

"Yeah. A little beat up, but nothing serious. My car, though . . . it's a mess."

"Who'd you run into?" I asked.

"Someone hit me, Connor. You know I can handle a car." He sounded insulted. "Guy ran a red light while yapping on his cell."

"Where are you?"

"Garcia Avenue and Twenty-second. By that strip mall. Will Dad be home soon?"

"Called a little while ago. He's running late at the lab."

"Call him. Tell him to meet me here. I'm waiting for the tow truck."

I called Dad's office and told him where to meet James. Then Kathleen and I sat on the sofa to wait for them to get home. I wasn't surprised that James had been in an accident. What astonished me was that it happened on a sunny afternoon and no racing was involved.

James and my father showed up later. James was cut and bruised, but mainly rattled about the demise of his car, which a scrapyard operator had hauled off in a symphony of metallic groans and skid marks.

My parents barely even got upset once they knew James was fine. I guess after what happened on Will's roof, a smashed Camaro is incidental.

"I've paid my dad almost everything I owe him," I told Mr. Driver.

"Really?" He flipped through my file and made a notation. "Bet it'll feel good to get that monkey off your back."

"Yeah. He's not pressuring me for it, but I want to be in the clear."

"Are you going to quit your job when your financial obligation has been met?"

"No. I like working at Manulet's, and it'll be nice to have some money."

"You'll still be on probation until you're eighteen. You remember that, don't you?"

"Yes."

"And if you get into any trouble, however trivial, they can yank your plea agreement?"

"Yes, I know. I'm careful." I swept to the back of my consciousness the reckless nights in James's Camaro.

SHOAL

My island receded into its ocean of glass. Quicksilver still visited me there, but he had to hover in the air because there was no longer enough room for both of us.

GARDEN PLOT

After school, I walked into the kitchen and rooted around in the refrigerator for something to eat.

"Connor?"

"Yeah, Mom?"

"Are you working this afternoon?"

"No . . . can I have this?" I pulled out a plastic container of leftovers.

"Yes. I thought you might give me a hand."

"Doing what?"

"My seedlings are ready to go into the ground."

"Yeah, I'll help." I stuck the food in the microwave and fished a fork out of the dishwasher. "Lemme eat first, okay?"

I met my mother on the back porch. Her flats of seedlings were lined up on the walk. She was dumping large bags of cow manure and peat moss into the garden plot to enrich the dirt.

"Here, Mom, I'll do that," I offered. Once all the sacks were emptied, I began spading the soil.

Mom was raking through the part of the garden I'd finished churning, fishing out weeds and roots and tossing them into a five-gallon bucket. A cool breeze ruffled the trees. We fell into a rhythm, not talking. I could smell the richness of the earth, a scent that always took me back to my early childhood. I remembered other springtimes, other gardens.

I jammed the shovel's blade into the earth. "I'm done," I said. "I'll take over raking if you get us something to drink."

When she returned with glasses of iced tea, we sat side by side on the steps.

"This is one of my favorite activities every year," my mother said. "I like that you share it with me."

"I like it, too, Mom. Guess it's a tradition, huh?"

She smiled. "A nice one . . . although the tables have certainly turned. Remember when I was the one who did the heavy work?"

I laughed. "I remember when you did all the work. You sure were patient. I bet you could have done the job in half the time without my help."

"It wouldn't have been nearly as much fun." She went

into the house to refill our glasses. When she returned, she said, "Sure has been a roller coaster these last months, hasn't it?"

"You mean since Daniel?"

"Yes, I guess I do."

"It'll never be over, will it, Mom?"

She set her glass on the step. "Not over, really. But you can let something build you up or break you down. I wasn't sure which way you were going."

"I'm okay."

"I think you are," she said. I could feel her looking at me. "I hope you are."

I gazed at the freshly prepared earth, following the lines and patterns left by the rake. "I'm not the same person I was then."

"No one is the same."

"The person I am now . . . I'd walk away."

She put her arm around my shoulder and leaned against me. "I believe you would."

We planted the seedlings, carefully spacing them and covering them with soil. While my mother put away the tools and plastic flats, I mulched the plants with oak leaves from the yard. We were standing to the side, admiring our work, when Kathleen swerved up on her bicycle with her softball glove dangling from the handlebar. "You did it without me," she cried. "You should have waited until I got off practice."

My mother smiled. "It was just Connor and me this

time, sweetheart. But there'll be plenty of other jobs—weeding and watering and cutting flowers. You can be our official flower arranger. How about that?"

Kathleen kicked at the grass with the toe of her softball cleats. "That'd be okay, I guess." She looked at me. "Hey, Connor, wanna shag balls?"

"That'd be okay, I guess," I replied, winking at her.

CONFRONTATION

Elwood was at the employee entrance to Manulet's when I got to work. "Connor," he said before I punched in, and signaled me to follow him. His clear blue eyes were dark that day. We went to the building maintenance shed next to the loading dock. He pulled his keys from his pants pocket and sprung the padlock. As he slid open the door, he motioned me inside.

The small corrugated aluminum building was cluttered with the usual stuff—brooms, mops, buckets, half-empty paint cans, a lawn mower, two ten-gallon gas containers, broken shelving units, an obsolete cash register, and a couple of rusty toolboxes. Then I saw the merchandise piled against the back wall. Electric hedge trimmers, leaf blowers,

Weed Eaters, a carton of hummingbird feeders, high-end lawn ornaments, three cases of expensive wind chimes, pruners, and a stack of tabletop fountains. All stuff from my department.

Elwood stepped into the shed behind me. "Wanna explain this?" he asked, gesturing toward the back wall.

I looked at him, puzzled. "Um . . . looks like stuff from the garden pavilion. What's it doing here?"

"That I can explain. I moved it. What I'd like to know is what my inventory was doing in the Dumpster."

"The Dumpster?" I felt a glacier sweep over me as I realized Elwood believed I had something to do with whatever was happening.

"Yes, Connor, the Dumpster. And not just tossed in like garbage. Wrapped in sheets of Visqueen and covered with trash."

My legs went weak. My voice faltered. "El-Elwood, I don't know anything about it. I promise."

"George said you dumped the trash last night."

"Yeah. But I didn't put that other stuff in there."

Elwood's eyes bored into mine. "I like you, Connor. And I trusted you. But I'm a businessman. No one steals from me and gets away with it."

I backed up—the air between us was that charged. "Elwood, I didn't steal that stuff. I don't know anything about it." As I spoke, I imagined him calling Mr. Driver, and Mr. Driver having me arrested. I visualized my father, looking intensely disappointed, almost repulsed, and my mother, wounded by my betrayal. I thought of Ryan, and Daniel's mother, and Mr. Danescu hearing the news and drawing the obvious but erroneous conclusions.

Elwood stood before me with his arms crossed in front of him. "I rarely take on any of Layton's boys. Only five before you, and none of them screwed me over. In fact, not that it's any of your business, but George was one. And in the ten years he's been with me I've never had any reason to doubt him."

"Please, Elwood, it wasn't me."

"Then who?"

I didn't have to think long. Jesse. I remembered his wild stories and cavalier attitude. But he was friendly, open. No way he would steal from Elwood, would he? Still . . .

Maybe it was the ancient taboo against ratting out a friend, or my reluctance to say out loud what my heart felt, or my fear that accusing Jesse would strengthen the case against me since we were friends. But I couldn't bring myself to name names.

"How would I know? But it wasn't me," I said again.

"I want to believe you, Connor. But I don't want you here. Not till I get to the bottom of this. Go on home."

"So I'm fired?"

Elwood turned toward the shed door as he spoke. "Just go home. I want you off the premises."

"What's wrong with you? You look like hell," James said when I walked into the house.

"Nothing," I muttered, turning my head so that he wouldn't see my face. I'd been fighting tears since I left Manulet's. I wasn't sure if I was reacting to anger, fear, or shame.

He followed me into the backyard. "Thought you were working today."

"Well, I'm not."

"Jeez, Connor, you're shaking. What happened?"

I pushed my forehead into the trunk of our oak tree. Its rough surface calmed my nerves a little. "James, I'm in bad trouble. I don't know what to do."

"Can't be that bad."

"They'll throw me in jail. Oh, God, I can't go to jail."

"Connor, what'd you do?"

"Nothing. But Elwood thinks I did. Thinks I stole his stuff." And I recounted to James the whole nightmare at Manulet's.

"Did you?" he asked.

I turned to glare at James. "Of course I didn't. You think I'm that stupid?"

"No. But someone obviously did. Who do you suspect?"

"I'm not sure. . . . I could make a guess."

"I bet it was that kid Jesse. He's pretty slick."

"I have no proof, but when I think about it, it makes sense. I saw him at the Dumpster the other night, but I thought he was just taking an unofficial break . . .

sometimes he sneaks a smoke out back, so I didn't pay any attention. And it was dusk—hard to see—so he could've been up to anything. I'm scared, James. I don't know what to do."

"Kick his ass."

"Believe me, I'd like to. But I mean about Elwood. He thinks I'm a thief."

James leaned against the tree. "Tell Dad," he said quietly after a while. "Ask for his help."

His suggestion was so outlandish I almost laughed. No way would I tell my father. "Right. Remember how he freaked out when he caught us breaking curfew? I can just imagine how he'd react to this."

RICOCHET

I climbed the fire escape of Will's building. No one took notice of me. Standing there on the roof, it all flooded over me in waves. I was chilled.

The abandoned chest of drawers that shielded the gun was still there, its veneer peeling from exposure to the weather. I walked the perimeter of the roof. I saw the sidewalk below, cracked and dirty. I saw the clouds above, a celebration.

I strayed to the place—the exact place—where it happened.

The place where we played that most dangerous, evil, irresponsible, murderous game. The air there was thick, so thick that it held me back, and I had to force my way through. I sat where I sat that night. I was scalded. I closed my eyes and remembered. I felt Ryan, Will, and Daniel there with me. I smelled the spent cartridge that spewed its chemicals into the air. I heard echoes and explosions ringing in my ears.

I remembered Daniel turning away from Will; the gun in Will's hand; the horrible jolt when the bullet made contact with Daniel's skull, ripping the world wide open; the wasted dreams as Daniel lay unmoving on the roof.

And Will shoving the gun into Daniel's pocket and smiling; and Ryan screaming and Daniel lying motionless in the starlight. I don't know what I was doing—praying, wishing, hoping, dreading, shouting, sinking, losing, dying.

FRIDAY EVENING

"Just got off work," Jesse said, leaning in the doorway. "You're the talk of the hardware store. You fooled everyone. They all said you seemed so innocent."

"Shut up, would you," I hissed, shoving him and

stepping outside before pulling the door closed. "The last thing I need is for my parents to get wind of this."

"Chill, man. They'll find out eventually. George says Elwood's going to report you."

"But I didn't do it. And if Elwood turns me in I'm going straight to jail. I'm on probation."

"Probation? What for?"

"Long story. One I'm not telling you. But Jesse, I'm not gonna let myself get busted for what you did, even if it was just one of your Robin Hood stunts."

"Me?"

"You."

"It's *you* they're looking at. You're the one who works in the garden center, Connor. The evidence points at you."

"Then they're looking at the wrong evidence. At the wrong person."

His wounded expression caused my certainty of his guilt to waver. "I wouldn't steal from Elwood," he protested. "I may pull a few pranks, but it's all harmless."

"This is no prank, Jesse."

"Doesn't matter. You're the one in the hot seat," he replied lightly with a hint of a sneer in his words. "And, apparently, you've been busted before. You ought to be used to it." He laughed, as if it was all a joke.

"Go to hell, Jesse."

"You're mad?" he asked, his tone oddly incredulous.

"Get out of here." I shoved him in the chest with my open hand. I expected him to come at me—hoped he would. I wanted to tear him apart. But something in my face must have warned him because he walked backward three or four steps before turning toward his car.

LINKS IN THE CHAIN

It was the wee hours of the morning. Everyone was sleeping. I could hear Trent inhaling and exhaling in his bed.

I couldn't stop thinking about the situation at Manulet's and wished Daniel was around. He'd always been good at talking me through whatever disaster I found myself party to. I thought of the things we once counted as troubles. They were now so ridiculously petty that I felt foolish.

I turned on the hall light. It flowed through the bedroom door, spilling onto my chest of drawers. I slid the top drawer open and took out the grocery bag of Daniel's things, remembering the day his mother brought them to me. This was the first time I had looked at them. I sat on the floor, letting my fingers absorb their energy. They were tangible things, but for me they were links to the intangibles of Daniel—the things that could not be named or categorized.

I held the pottery bird Daniel made at day camp when we were nine. It felt cold and heavy in my hands. Its long, curved beak and huge feet were humorous. I liked the heaviness of Daniel's bird. The joy of it.

It took me back to those muggy summer afternoons at the park. I had made a clumsy frog with big webbed feet and a pink tongue hanging out of its mouth. A blob of a fat black fly sat boldly on the tip of the frog's tongue. My father had taken it to his office at the lab. I wondered if it was still perched on his desk.

I flipped through a stack of photographs: Daniel and me with our hair wet from the ocean and salt crusted on our flesh. Of us at the end-of-the-season baseball party when we were in fifth grade, grinning, our hats turned backward and our jerseys inside out. Dressed in Halloween costumes. Sweaty and dirty from playing capture the flag with the kids from Daniel's block. Jazzed up for the eighth-grade dance at the end of middle school, where neither of us found the nerve to actually dance with any of the girls.

I pulled Daniel's Bob Marley T-shirt over my head and slipped my arms into the sleeves. It was tight through the shoulders and too short. I stripped it off, deciding to give it to Kathleen. I knew she'd appreciate having something of Daniel's.

I looked at an envelope labeled STITCHES. I would have recognized that careless penmanship anywhere as Daniel's. I poured a handful of twisted black threads, looking like tiny dead flies, into my palm. Daniel had saved the stitches they removed from his head after our bicycle collision at the reservoir. Only Daniel would have saved his stitches, a sort of trophy of our adventure. I held them up to the hall light. I knew they contained the most essential and primal secrets of Daniel because I could see flecks of dried blood stuck to the fibers.

I would miss Daniel forever. Knew that no wish, no magic, no prayer would allow him to stand beside me again.

SHADES OF GRAY

Quicksilver brought Truth to me some nights. At first he held it out like a prize, but I was afraid to take it. Then he sang my secret name and put Truth into my hands. I ran my fingers over its surface. In places it was rough and scratched my flesh. In other places it was as smooth as a breeze. Truth glowed brightly. It smelled of jasmine and blood and the ocean. But I was perplexed: Each time I held Truth, its colors and textures were different. But never was Truth black or white.

One bitter arctic night, the dragon king came to me as I

shivered alone on my island. He held Truth out to me. I reached for it, but the cold made my hands clumsy. Truth slipped from my fingers and slammed into the ice, fracturing into pieces and spilling its colors.

IDENTITY THEFT

I stopped dead at the foot of the bridge, my body frozen, my stomach twisting inside me. A guy in a leather jacket was leaning against the railing in the center, calling to someone below in a small boat. It was him. It had to be. Will—with his trademark posture, intonation of voice, and barking laughter. But what was he doing there—had he been released from prison because of some loophole? Escaped? Somehow scammed his way out?

I wanted to flee. Couldn't possibly face him. I felt as if I'd been plunged into icy water.

He raised his hand and ruffled his hair. That same nervous gesture I remembered.

I retraced my steps to the corner. Then I turned again to work out the visual puzzle of Will and what he was doing there. Suddenly I knew that I *had* to face him. That if I let his presence intimidate me I'd remember that moment with shame and regret for the rest of my life.

All at once, determination surged through me. I felt solid. I would no longer allow Will, with his devil's eyes and corrupt voice, to dominate me. I realized he had been haunting me since that one vile night. But he was nobody without a weapon in his hand. Just an angry, deranged teenager—even a little fragile. My hatred and loathing drained away.

I walked back toward the bridge. I touched the plastic gator in my pocket. I didn't know what Will and I had to say to each other. The only thing we had ever shared was the worst moment of my life. I glanced at the boat below. The lone occupant held a fishing rod. He was shading his eyes against the bright sun as he stared up at Will while the two of them talked. My gaze shifted back to Will, who was no more than twenty feet away. I slowed my pace, pondering what to say. "Will," I called, my voice steadier than I had expected. It was devoid of fear or retreat.

He pushed himself away from the railing and turned toward me. Seeing him straight on, I realized he wasn't Will after all. His features were sharper and his eyes more deep-set. He was older—probably in his twenties.

"Sorry, thought you were someone else," I said.

"No problem," answered the guy. "Take it easy," he called to the man below.

I watched him walk away. To have found the grit to

face Will and then be disappointed left me vaguely deflated, but also stronger, bolder.

ALMOST

I didn't want to approach the building. Didn't want my coworkers to stare at me. I couldn't believe less than a week had passed since the theft at Manulet's. It felt like eternity. One afternoon while I was at Mr. Danescu's, Elwood left a message with James that he wanted to see me. I considered blowing him off completely. Then I thought of Mr. Driver, who'd trusted me—who'd put his friendship with Elwood on the line to give me a break.

I leaned my bicycle against the fence and brushed my hands on my jeans before heading for the building. "I'm supposed to see Elwood," I said to the first employee I saw. "He here?"

"In his office," came the girl's noncommittal reply.

As I walked past the checkout counters at the front of the store, I looked neither right nor left. I didn't want to gauge the reactions of my coworkers there. I saw Elwood through the glass in his office door. He sat behind his desk talking on the phone and doodling on a scratch pad. I knocked on the window. He looked up, then waved me in. I closed the door and stood awkwardly in front of it, waiting. "Lemme call you back," Elwood said, and hung up the phone. He stood and reached across the desk to shake my hand. I tried to read his handshake and body language—to learn from them the reason for this meeting. "Please sit down, Connor."

There was a chair on the opposite side of the desk. I pulled it out to perch on the edge. I didn't meet Elwood's eyes. Instead I looked around the small disorderly room, taking in the stains on the Sheetrock, the nicks and scratches on the furniture, the paint can of pencils and pens on the desk, the computer monitor with its wallpaper of interlocking gears.

Elwood cleared his throat. "I appreciate you coming. Wasn't sure you'd show."

"Almost didn't," I mumbled, now studying the spots on the floor, connecting them to form constellations as the ancients did with the stars. The shape of a dancing gypsy girl emerged.

"I don't blame you. You doing okay?"

"I've been better." A great white shark appeared next to my left foot.

"I imagine you have." A spiraled constellation like a nautilus shell materialized near the doorway.

Elwood shifted in his seat. I heard his chair scrape the

floor. He cleared his throat again. "I misjudged you, Connor. Jumped to conclusions based on only the obvious evidence. Should've trusted my instincts, which told me you weren't involved. I'm sorry."

Surprised, I looked up. Elwood's eyes were on mine. He glanced away first. "So now you think I'm innocent?" I asked.

"I know you are. You have Layton to thank for that. Had some friends in law enforcement compare the fingerprints from your file to the ones on the merchandise. Yours weren't on the stolen inventory or the plastic it was wrapped in."

I felt immense relief. "I told you I didn't do it." I wondered if I sounded petulant or accusing. I felt the urge to rave, but held my tongue.

"I know, Connor."

"So who did?"

Again he looked me in the eyes. "Jesse."

"Jesse," I said flatly after a noticeable pause.

"Yes. His prints were on all the stuff. When confronted, he admitted a pal of his was selling the merchandise at the flea market and giving him a cut."

I didn't say anything.

"Kinda left you swinging in the wind, didn't he?"

A snapshot of Jesse smiling lazily while I dangled from the gallows flashed through my mind. I'd accepted him as a friend. And now I compared him to Will. One glance at Will was a warning—you knew he was dangerous. Jesse was different—friendly and funny and openhearted. I hadn't thought anyone could be more corrupt than Will, but Jesse was. The blade of a smile digs in more deeply and slices more sharply than that of a sneer.

Then I thought of Stewart, who in his quiet way had been my friend for a long time without me realizing it. I remembered things I'd confided to him. I'd never actually felt close enough to Jesse to tell him the story of Daniel's shooting or any of my other secrets. So maybe, in spite of his appeal, I'd never truly trusted him—never really connected with him.

"Connor?"

I focused my eyes, suddenly aware that Elwood had been speaking. "I'm sorry. What did you say?"

He smiled his Travis Tritt smile. "I asked if you'd come back. With a pay raise and a genuine apology."

Pride, like a cartoon devil standing on my shoulder, urged me to leave in righteous indignation. Reason, the animated angel on my other shoulder, argued in favor of graciously accepting Elwood's offer. I paused for a moment. I was wounded by Elwood's mistrust even though I could understand it. I *was* the obvious suspect. But I did like my job at Manulet's. It represented an independence I'd never had before, as well as a weekly paycheck. It was a struggle. I closed my eyes, seeking an answer. Quicksilver flashed past whispering that word again—*forgiveness*. I reached across the desk to shake Elwood's hand. "Yessir, I'd like to come back. With the pay raise. Don't forget the pay raise."

I left Manulet's and went to the reservoir. The sky slowly darkened. The water was as still as a mirror. Was I so desperate for a friend I hadn't seen through Jesse, I wondered, or would anyone have been suckered by him? I hoped it was the latter, the first option being too pathetic to ponder.

I arrived home later, a paradox of emotions charging through me. Relief and anger and exhilaration and resentment. Exhausted, but too agitated for sleep, I walked to the window and stared into the yard.

"You watching the meteor shower?" my father asked.

"What?"

"There's a meteor shower tonight—God's own fireworks display." His voice betrayed his reverence at this spectacular event. I followed him out the back door. We sat side by side at the picnic table.

I looked at the sky. There was no moon at all. Just the stars, my father, and me. "Hey, Dad? I'm sorry. I'm really sorry about everything."

He sighed, then looked at me. "I know, son. Me too. I'm sorry too. We've all made mistakes." He threw his arm over my shoulder. That was the first time he had touched me since the night of my apocalypse.

Then my father, the scientist, outlined for me the chemical reactions in the burning gaseous fireballs above that allowed the night to explode. But I knew, in spite of his technical knowledge, that the sky that night was awash with the fire of the dragon king.

PHOSPHORUS

Exactly why I felt strange when I went to my next appointment with Mr. Driver, I can't say. For some reason I was embarrassed and humbled. He smiled when I appeared in the doorway of his cubicle. "Hello, Connor," he said softly.

"Hi." I sat across from him. "I'm not fired anymore."

"I know."

"Thanks for what you did."

"It's my job. If it had come out the other way, I'd have turned you in. It's not personal, Connor. I like you. But it's my job."

"Thanks just the same," I said softly.

"You're welcome."

I looked at my hands in my lap. "It was awful, getting sent away like that. People thinking it was me."

"I'm sure it was."

"People think because something happened once, I'm tainted for life."

"Not really. Most people understand and move on. But that's something you'll have to come to terms with."

"Yeah, I know. But it follows me."

"Everyone has demons, Connor," he said slowly, "although not everyone calls them by that name. Write them away. My demons could not abide words. The more I wrote about them, the weaker they became, until one day they were only harmless shadows." He pushed a thin wisp of hair from his forehead. "I'll admit that they occasionally slip back into my life, but I've learned to deal with them."

TOTE THE WEARY LOAD

I walked across the yard scanning the sheet music for the new piece Mr. Danescu had assigned. James bellowed out a rebel yell, jumped from the porch, and slammed me to the ground. "Hey, little wimp," he said, laughing. My backpack flew off in one direction and my instrument case in the opposite. I heard the music folio crumple and tear and won-dered how I'd explain that one when I showed up for my next lesson. "So you got your job back?"

"Yeah," I said as I grappled to get away.

"Awesome."

"Yeah."

James and I wrestled and rolled and snarled at each other, both confident that the end result would follow the usual pattern—me pinned to the ground and forced to say uncle before James released me. We had a lifetime history of this brotherly scuffling. Sometimes it was mostly friendly, sometimes it masked the natural animosity that comes of living together.

I pushed him away and rolled to my knees, and then, somehow, he was pinned. I anchored my forearm across his throat and said, "What do you say, wussboy?"

James struggled, but my hold on him was solid.

"Well?" I bore down on his throat just a shade harder.

He kicked and thrashed helplessly.

"What do you say?" I asked again.

"Uncle," he muttered, and I released him.

He sat up and rubbed his throat, smiling all the while. "Damn, little brother, when'd you get so buff?"

"What are you talking about?"

"You've never whupped me like that before. Look at your shoulders and arms. When did that happen?"

I shrugged and grinned. "I guess that's how it is when you actually work for a living. Maybe if you did something more than tear ticket stubs and sell popcorn I wouldn't have beaten you."

He laughed. "Actually, I let you win."

"Sure you did."

GLAZED

Holding Daniel's pottery bird, I walked across the hall to my parents' bedroom. My father was getting ready to take Kathleen to her softball game. I sat on the bed, watching him pull a clean T-shirt over his head. "Dad?"

"Yes?"

I held out the bird. "This was Daniel's. He made it the same summer I made that frog. Remember that frog? Do you still have it?"

He took the bird from my hand and examined it. "Yes, it's on my desk at work."

I exhaled with relief. Before now, I hadn't realized how important it was to me that the clay frog was still squatting patiently in his lab.

"Do you want it back?" He handed me Daniel's bird.

"The frog? No. I was just wondering about it. I'm glad you still have it."

"Me too. I always liked that frog." He checked his watch. "Why don't you go to Kathleen's game with us?"

"Okay."

"But not barefooted. Go put on some shoes."

"Hey, Dad . . . thanks."

CHORD

I stood in the doorway, reflecting on the events of the past months. On the many ways I'd changed—some for the better, some not. I was warier now—a little jaded. I still knew something valuable was lost when I put that gun to my head. Something irretrievable. But something was learned, too. A trade-off. Not an even trade, but a trade.

After looking up the number, I picked up the phone and dialed.

"Hi, Stewart. It's Connor."

"Hey. What's up?" I'd never called Stewart before, but he didn't seem to find it strange.

"I'm playing at an art opening at the cultural center Saturday night. Thought you might want to come. We can play those duets we've been doing in class."

"Saturday night? Sure. Do I have to wear a tie?"

"Yeah."

THE FINAL MOVEMENT

After the theft at Manulet's, I went back to my composition "Ladder of Glass." I saw and felt things differently now. I played through the first and second movements with ease. They'd become part of who I was. Suddenly, the third movement came to me. It was not the lament or crescendo or joyous song I had attempted to write before. It was a wild dance of leaping from rung to rung, the occasional rung shattering beneath my weight. I played it through, made revisions, and played it through again. Yes, that was it. There was no final high or low, no dramatic final scene—everything depended only on the will to keep on dancing.

I spent the day with Uncle Pete in his studio. He was busy painting and had John Lee Hooker playing in the background. That's what Uncle Pete usually listened to when he painted—the blues. The studio smelled of paint and linseed oil and lemongrass tea. The morning sun streamed through the skylights.

I watched Uncle Pete from across the room. He didn't talk while he painted, and I could see that he was adrift in his work. He used paintbrushes of different sizes, layering the paint on the canvas, color on color, varying the length and direction of the brushstrokes to create a rich, textured surface. Watching him, I was hypnotized by his movements, by the power of his strokes, the power to alter an existence.

I had come to think of my life as a canvas, and all my choices and experiences as brushstrokes on that canvas. Some of the brushstrokes were fearsome or violent; others were pure or joyous or whimsical. Some were tears and scars; others were embraces.

I looked back over my past. There were brushstrokes that at one time seemed a significant part of the composition, but had been painted out completely. They had lost their importance. Others would remain forever, but their character could be altered by the colors that surrounded them or crossed over them.

I wondered how I could alter the pain of Daniel's brush-strokes, the shame and fears of my own. What colors should I use, and which brushes?

Sunlight tumbling through the skylights cast shadows at new angles around the studio. Uncle Pete sighed and used a greasy rag soaked in solvent to remove the paint from his hands.

AND THEN

I stood on the bridge watching the current. A breeze ruffled the water and scattered the clouds reflected there. I saw a flash of ultramarine light and felt the breath of the dragon king on my neck as he bade me a final farewell and faded away.

ABOUT THE AUTHOR

Julie Gonzalez lives in Pensacola, Florida, with her husband, Eric, and their four children. Her first novel, *Wings*, won the Delacorte Press Prize for a First Young Adult Novel.